"*Strange Love* is a hard book to put down—an effect which might take some by surprise: after all, these first-person stories are serial episodes in the love life of a woman writer in middle age, who already has the room of her own and the first book, but wants—fiercely—a love of her own into the bargain. Why is this so fascinating? First, Lisa Lenzo writes (has always written) with a rare directness and candor, not so much about sex (although sex is definitely part of the deal, in *Strange Love*) as about the hunger for attachment, and the lengths to which a strong and independent woman might go to satisfy it. Second, there's something at once shocking and deeply familiar about the parade of interesting yet damaged men who present themselves to a woman over forty in the market for a second marriage. Lenzo's portraits of Annie and her men are polished, raw, infuriating, and sympathetic, all at the same time."

JAIMY GORDON
National Book Award–winning author of *Lord of Misrule*

"The narrative of a conventional novel also becomes the design of its main character's life. But in Lisa Lenzo's *Strange Love*—a novel-in-stories—her character, Annie, who yearns for love to shape her life, finds love to be elusive and all but shapeless. It is that kind of challenging honesty that informs and distinguishes this intimate book along with Lenzo's dependably wise humor, her vivid and credible character portraits, and her charming way with anecdotes—in other words, with her consummate skill as a storyteller."

STUART DYBEK
author of *I Sailed with Magellan*

"Everybody in this book is hungry for love, and nobody is hungrier than Annie Zito, but this divorced mother never loses her head and only rarely considers murder. Annie's voice beguiles us with the details of doomed relationships with men who turn out to be eccentrics, neurotics, and commitment-phobics, as well as those who simply decide they want somebody else. 'Weirdos and whackos,' declares Annie's daughter Marly, who sometimes delights us with her forthrightness and at other times frightens us with her vulnerability as she deals with friends and lovers in her own life. And while this mother-daughter relationship is bumpy at turns, its constancy provides counterpoint to their romantic struggles. These stories will surprise you with their intensity and intimacy, and Lenzo's language will mesmerize you."

BONNIE JO CAMPBELL
bestselling author of Once Upon a River and National Book Award finalist of American Salvage (Wayne State University Press, 2009)

"Beyond the map lies the territory within, and the characters that reside in Lisa Lenzo's rural Michigan charm with their daredevil imperative to love and lose and to seek love yet again. With the gravity and momentum of a novel, and the intensity and focus of the short story, Strange Love is pitch-perfect, a blend of comedy and pathos, folly and hope, simultaneously small-town and so big-hearted that I did not, upon turning the final page, want this book to end. A storyteller of unusual powers."

JACK DRISCOLL
author of The World of a Few Minutes Ago (Wayne State University Press, 2012)

Strange
Love

Strange
Love

stories by LISA LENZO

WAYNE STATE UNIVERSITY PRESS   Detroit

18   17   16   15   14   5   4   3   2   1

ISBN 978-0-8143-4017-2 (paperback) / ISBN 978-0-8143-4018-9 (e-book)

Library of Congress Control Number: 2013950623

∞

Publication of this book was made possible by a generous gift
from The Meijer Foundation.

Designed and typeset by Charlie Sharp, Sharp Des!gns
Composed in Novel Pro

For Cloey
and
For Charlie

CONTENTS

Still Life   3

17   Aliens

Fishing   29

61   Strays

Loveland Pass   77

113   Flames

Strange Love   139

177   Hands

Love Again   195

229
ACKNOWLEDGMENTS

Strange Love

Still Life

I'm supposed to be studying at my kitchen table, which in the two years since my divorce has doubled as my desk, but as the evening wears on, I push aside my textbooks, pick up *Single File*—the local personal ad paper—and start leafing through the men. One guy in a ten-gallon claims to be a cowboy, although in this part of Michigan, the main herd animals are tourists, not cattle. Another man, with eyes like iron, writes that he can **show wommin a lotta fun**. Yet another, under "**Last Book Read**," has filled in **n/a**. But there are a few—men who grow basil and tomatoes and bake bread and read books—whom I think I might like to go out with, or date.

Date. Go out. Those words still seem strange. I moved in with Ray, whom I later married, when I was only eighteen and never really dated before then. I'd just get to know some boy at school, and we'd hang out at each other's houses and the houses of friends and at the park near where I lived. I'd had sex and pizza with three different boyfriends before I met my husband, but never had some date driven up to my door and taken me out to dinner. Once my favorite boyfriend and I biked to an art fair, and another time this same boy and I borrowed my parents' car to pick apples—and then I crashed the car; I pulled out into traffic and totaled my parents' new Fiat, so the apple picking never came off. Remembering that accident—the shocking jolt and crunch of metal, the frantic beating of my heart—makes me want to just forget this whole dating idea. Who knows what kind of damage I might cause or invite? I've been trying to date since soon after my divorce, but I still feel almost entirely out-of-step. In the meantime, my ex-husband seems to be striding just fine. He recently told me that he is getting remarried, and our daughter drew a picture of the upcoming event: a girl circled by flowers beside a bear holding a ring, beneath which Marly had written that she will be the **flowr girl** and the **ring bear** because her dad and Dora are **getting marred**. I'd like to get married again, too. Maybe. If I can keep the marring to a minimum.

I lean back in my chair and put my bare feet up on my kitchen table. A couple of hours ago, Marly heard me telling a friend over the phone that I was thinking of finding a boyfriend through a personal ad. "What about Matt?" Marly asked, looking up from her stuffed tiger and stuffed cat, which were propped against the kitchen wall next to tiny cups of tea. "I thought Matt was your boyfriend."

"Well, he's not," I answered. "Matt is just someone I've gone out with a couple of times."

Matt is a fellow grad student in the creative writing

program at Western Michigan. He is twenty-two, plenty old enough to drink coffee or even beer, yet for some reason we have drunk just Cokes together, twice. I'm only thirty-one, but on my second date with Matt I felt forty-one or even fifty. That night I dreamed my hair had turned gray and my face had shrunk into wrinkles, but I was wearing the pink dotted sundress I felt too old for when I was eight.

Besides Matt, I've had a few other rendezvous that might be called dates, plus a couple of shaky relationships—one with a married man who lives in Grand Haven, thirty miles north of my little apartment, and one with a singer-songwriter from the music program at Western. Neither of these relationships had lasted long or was very satisfying; what kept me involved were my fantasies of the future: the married man's divorce and our subsequent marriage (he still sends me postcards now and then, but that's it) and the musician's ambivalent love blossoming into commitment (he took off at the end of the semester to sing on streetcorners in California and called me just once, from the road at two A.M., too drunk to know, or at least to get across, where it was that he was calling from).

Nor have my few "dates" turned out the way I had hoped. A man I met in a bar came over to my apartment for our first date on the night his father died. Earlier, we had talked about going out to hear music, but when I answered my door the man leaned against the frame and said, "My father is dying—can I use your phone?" I let him in and showed him the phone, and he sat down at the dresser I share with my daughter and dialed his mother in Florida. Then he said, "Oh no. Oh no." I retreated into my kitchen to make tea, wondering if there was something else I should be doing. I thought of offering him a beer, but he already reeked of beer. I had talked to this man just three times, once at the bar and then twice on the phone, and now here he was on my phone, softly sobbing.

I returned to him with a mug of tea—he had hung up and stopped crying by then—and after he talked to me about his father and then about himself, he began inquiring about me and my life: "Tell me about yourself," he kept saying, which made me feel as if I were on The Dating Game. My usual chatty nature folded further and further inward, until, at ten o'clock, the man leapt up to go. I had been smiling, trying to see the evening in its best light; I walked him to the door noticing the shabbiness of my linoleum, whose pattern of blue, red, and silver streaks on pale yellow I'd always liked until that moment. As soon as the door closed, I put my head down on my kitchen counter.

My most recent "date," with a man I met at a contra dance, had gone even worse. As I was about to go to bed with him on our second evening alone together, I realized that I didn't really even want to hold his hand. I'd had sex with him after he brought me home from our first date, and I'd assumed that I'd want to have sex with him again, but when he showed up on that second night, I realized, too late, that I had made a mistake: he was standing in my doorway like a homeless person, his clothes for the following day in one paper bag and his dinner in another, and, before I could think of how to react, he was sitting in my kitchen, eating moo-shu pork at my table, and then saying we had to get up early for work, and wasn't it time for bed?

At first I tried to convince myself that I hadn't changed my mind. But as I slowly peeled off my clothes, I couldn't stop thinking about the men I in some ways still loved: the married man who continued to write postcards, the music student who had taken off for California, the boy I had crashed a car with in high school. Meanwhile, this man whom I met at a contra dance had finished stripping, and all six feet and nearly two hundred muscular pounds of him were waiting for me under my covers. I shouldn't have let things get so far so fast, I thought. Why had this seemed so uncomplicated in high school? I would go through with it, then never let something like this happen again.

But as I stood on the far side of my combination bedroom-living room, removing the second of my three layers of winter clothing, the contra dance man asked me what was taking me so long. I hesitated the length of two heartbeats. Then I told him the truth. "Well," I said, trying to gently say words that cannot be gently spoken, "I've just realized that I'm not sure if I want to sleep with you."

The man jumped up, pulled on his clothes, and stormed out of my apartment. The following day, he called me a half-dozen times, hanging up each time without saying a word after I said hello. He didn't hang up right away—he let a little silence pass first; enough for me to remember, as if I could let it slip my mind, that there was a man out there whom I had hurt who knew where to find me.

After he called at eleven P.M.—he'd called every hour since seven P.M.—I unplugged my phone and threw my weight against my refrigerator and shoved it from its corner until it blocked my apartment door.

⁓

GIVEN THOSE TWO MISHAPS, I might have decided to steer clear of dating strangers, but there's a difference between meeting men at a bar or a dance and meeting them through an ad: when using the personal-ad route, initial contact is indirect. The men who respond to my profile will write me or leave a voice mail by a double-blind method; we won't meet in person right away, and our addresses, phone numbers, and last names won't be revealed to each other unless and until we reveal them ourselves. This controlled anonymity suits me fine. I don't want any more men's fathers dying on my doorstep, or another man ending up in my bed by mistake. I've moved my refrigerator back into its corner, but ever since that night it has emitted piercing cheeps at odd intervals, like the cries of a wounded bird.

The bird cry sounds suddenly as I sit contemplating men at my kitchen table, a high-pitched, mournful noise that also carries a note of warning, as if to remind me to be careful, that people can get hurt—me, as well as the man who stripped himself naked and whom I then turned away.

I get up from my chair and put on some water for tea. My kitchen is small, considering it's where Marly and I eat, where I type up my papers for school, where, when Marly is asleep in the next room, as she is now, I study and read. The refrigerator, cupboards, and walls are covered with Marly's artwork and photos of landscapes that I cut from last year's calendar. Marly's drawings are bright and cheery—girls dressed in blue and yellow with hair streaming to their waists, sunny skies and rainbows and apple trees in bloom—and the landscapes are like extra windows, windows with spectacular views: two show mountain vistas; another, a wilderness lake; and the last is of an ocean beach like the Lake Michigan shore that lies just three miles from here. The drawings and especially the landscapes open up the apartment; they make it seem larger than it is. As does the Matisse poster I bought and taped to the wall near the chair where I always sit.

The poster is of a still life: a room with a wooden table and chair, a vase of red peonies, a plate of peaches, and a book. The book lies open on the table, and it looks—it feels—as if someone has just gotten up and will return and resume reading at any moment. I imagine the interrupted reader to be a man, a formal but friendly man who spends long stretches absorbed in books. He has stood up to answer the door or to retrieve something from a part of his house not depicted in the poster. The man never comes into view, of course—not even a fraction of his hand or his sleeve ever crosses the edge of the poster—but he always seems very close, always on the verge of returning to the book and the room that lie within my sight.

Other times I forget all about this man and look into the poster as if the room there is another room of my own apartment. It is a room I will someday enter and inhabit. The vase of peonies will still be blooming when I reach them, and the book, still open and waiting. It's a book I'll want to read—a story collection or a novel. I often glance up at the tempting pages of the book in the poster while reading a dry text for school.

As I sit down with my mug of tea, bobbing the bag in the hot water, I think of returning to one of those texts—*Research and Writing*, or *The Family in Society*— and getting through a few more pages; instead I set down my mug, pull my chair close to my table, place my hands on the keyboard, and start typing.

Hair: **brown**; eyes: **hazel**; height: **5´4˝**. I stop. What does my height matter? But maybe it will, to a guy who is six feet seven. And if I scrutinize every particular, I'll never get the thing written. If my profile comes out lousy, I don't have to submit it. But the suggested format is stifling: **Things I do for Fun, Places I'd like to Go, My Favorite Vacation**. It would be better to write it in my own words, in longhand, and then edit the information. I turn off my computer and pick up my notebook. I'll take a sip of tea, then write the thing through without stopping.

The tea feels good in my mouth and throat—just the right strength, just the right heat; it slips in a straight, warm wave down to my stomach, where it spreads out and disappears. But the warmth at the back of my throat stays. I feel my eyes narrow like a cat's when it is pleased and look out at the other room of my apartment.

Marly has pulled her covers up past her chin, and her blond, wavy hair hides the rest of her face. She is curled up at the center of her bed, which in the daytime folds up into a small couch. This couch-bed takes up one side of the combination bedroom-living room. I sleep on a fabric-covered foam mattress on the floor across from Marly. The large dresser we share is placed between us and against a wall, with four drawers for me and two for Marly, since Marly's clothes are smaller and she keeps half of them at her father's house.

Besides this main room and the kitchen, there is only a tiny bathroom, but whenever my friends see the apartment for the first time, they look around at the walls for a doorway to another room. Twice friends have asked me where the other room was. I thought of pointing at the poster, but I didn't want to reveal the poster's private meaning or to turn it into a joke, and, anyway, I enjoyed my friends' surprise when I said that there wasn't any other room, that this was all there was to it. I didn't feel embarrassed. Neither did I feel poor. I'm a college student after all, as well as newly divorced, and, having grown up middle-class, I don't harbor a poor child's remembered shame. Whenever I do occasionally feel sorry for myself, I remind myself that I have heat, hot water, electricity, and so much food that sometimes some of it rots in my refrigerator, which is more than three-fourths of the world's people can claim. Most of the time I'm proud of myself for being content with so little. I am like a monk or a scholar; I have everything that is essential.

I pick up a pen. **I'm a student**, I write—I stare at the page—**I teach college part-time, and I drive for a bus company in the summer. I have an eight-year-old daughter who spends half of each week with her dad**. *And what with school, work, and my kid*, I think, *I don't have time for a man.* But I find myself being drawn to them, and them being drawn to me. Just yesterday I noticed an appealing man watching me at the Douglas beach. The man looked at me in a kind and interested way, and I felt like walking up to him. But what could I say? "Excuse me, but I noticed you looking at me appreciatively? I saw you checking me out?" And what if he turned out to be another mistake, a worse one, perhaps, than the ones I'd already made? He was likely married or otherwise spoken for anyway, as are the few men in my classes, except the very youngest and the terminally unattached, those afflicted, as my friend Nina likes to say, with serious commitment disorders.

I tap the end of the pen against my thigh. There are a lot of other things I could be doing right now. I could be starting a pot of soup for the coming week or making notes for my next paper. But the noise of chopping onions might wake Marly, and I'm in no mood for schoolwork; my brain has moved beyond that capacity and won't return to it until I've slept. I'm not sleepy yet, though—tired, but not sleepy.

Okay, I think, *let's break this down.* What does a personal ad consist of? A physical description, a list of interests, a character trait or two, mention of a job sometimes, and then a description of the kind of man that the woman is looking for. That last part is easy. I want someone who is intelligent and, of course, kind, someone easy-going, yet responsible, and preferably not too dour. I want someone who likes to talk and who likes to listen, who is confident but not an egomaniac, who can admit that he is wrong but isn't wrong very often, and who won't insist on a lot of my time, since I have so little to spare. Yet I do have some time—right now, for instance, I could be face-to-face with a man instead of thinking about how to find one.

I'm not writing anything down, I think. *Let's start at the beginning, and, really, this time, write the thing through. Don't worry about how it sounds—you can shorten it and fix it later. Pretend you're knocking out a paper that's due tomorrow.* I take another long sip of tea, swallow, and begin to write without thinking.

I'm 5' 4", 120 pounds, with hazel eyes and short brown hair. I'm a full-time grad student, a part-time bus driver, and the mother of an eight-year-old girl. I consider describing Marly—it seems heartless to mention her age and nothing else, nothing of her brightness, and . . . I push on. **I like to write, read, walk, dance, garden, swim, and canoe. But I don't have space for a garden anymore, and I never have time to canoe—I spend all my time going to school, working, and taking care of my child. I've seen only one movie in the last year, and I've gone dancing only twice. I do take one night off every week to sit around with my women friends and talk and eat dessert. I also take time off to walk by the lake, which is where I go instead of to church.**

I would make time for a man in my life. I'm loyal and stubborn and fierce. *Where did that word come from?* **I'm prickly and hard to please, too sensitive and too intense. I'm quiet until I start talking, and then you can't shut me up. My eyes**

scare men away—my vision is 20–10, sharper than perfect. Yet I don't see what I'm doing wrong. I'm looking for a man I can love and respect, but I'm not sure what kind of man that is, or if I'll know him when I find him. I want to be incredibly close, yet I also want to keep my distance. Sometimes I like sleeping alone and I think, *Why ruin this by adding a man?* Sometimes I still feel that rush sleeping alone that I did years ago when Marly was a baby and my husband went away to a conference for a week. Every night for a week I got to go to bed whenever I wanted to, and I could read in bed without having someone beside me asking me to turn off the light or sending out I'm-feeling-neglected vibes. That week of nights that my husband was away, I stopped reading and turned off the light at the exact moment I wanted to and felt no guilt. One night I got up again and walked through the house, like a panther let out of its cage.

I look up from my notebook and gaze at the poster. What I really want, I decide, is to be sitting at that table in the poster, reading that book, with those peonies beside me and quiet rooms beyond me. Outside, a garden with fruits and flowers—that's where the peonies have come from, I have cut them myself. I want time to read books leisurely, books of my own choosing. Yet I also want a man, a partner. But only if he has enough interests of his own to leave me plenty of time to myself, and if our house is as much mine as it is his—I felt like a prostitute in my marriage once love was gone, trading sex and cleaning and cooking for the roof over my head, and I felt so relieved and free on the day I finally left. I promised myself then that I would never again have sex with a man unless I really wanted to. I'd almost gone back on my promise to myself, with the man I met at the contra dance.

I look again at the poster, at the bright-red peonies with their bluish shadows, and at the dark-brown wooden table and the lighter, straight-backed wooden chair, and at the book lying open on the table's grainy surface. Suddenly I want to touch that table and to look at the book from up close. I have never done this—when I taped the poster to the wall, I only touched and looked at its edges, concerned only with hanging it straight. Now I stand and step up to the poster's surface.

At such close range, all illusion disappears: the poster's table is flat and slick, without texture or depth, and the pages of the book are an equally flat, depthless rectangle of white, gray, and black. The book's text isn't made up of actual words—just black, squiggly lines that are wholly unreadable, that were never meant to be read. Well, of course. I knew that. Yet I still feel disappointed.

I return to my chair and take a sip of my tea, which is cold now, but clean and sweet, and look out into the other room of my apartment. The room is dark, lit only by light falling in from the kitchen, a thick band of which crosses Marly at her feet.

Even though she's only in third grade and weighs less than fifty pounds, Marly has already entered the romantic arena. Last week during recess, three boys asked to be her boyfriend. Marly told the three to hold a footrace, and she would be the girlfriend of the winner. Marly wanted Jake to win, and he did.

"But Marly," I protested, "why didn't you just choose Jake, since he's the one you wanted?"

"I didn't want to hurt anyone's feelings," Marly said.

"But what if Jake had lost?"

"That's why I made them race. I knew Jake was the fastest."

If only she could stay that smart. And if love could stay that simple.

Marly is sleeping soundly on her little couch-bed, her skinny body curled up beneath the covers, her pale, perfect face nestled between a green blanket and her pillow. When I was her age, I had a normal bed and my own room, and I lived in a five-bedroom house with my mother *and* my father, as well as my four brothers. Yet Marly doesn't seem to feel deprived. The living room looks out onto a marshy backwater of the Kalamazoo River, and the morning light that comes in through its big, east-facing window gives getting up an element of pleasantness and even of grace. A couple of mornings ago, standing in her pajamas in the rosy light, Marly looked around the room, at the two makeshift beds and the single dresser and the tiny carpeted center, and said in a pleased voice, "We really *live* in our living room, don't we, Mom?"

"Yes, we do, honey," I answered, glad at that moment for everything we had and for everything that had brought us to this place.

Now the shade is drawn against the dark. It's a dirty off-white and torn along the bottom. *Go to bed*, I tell myself. But I remain seated. I clasp my hands in my lap, close my eyes, and turn my attention inward; I bend my head forward as if listening for the step of a deer and try to drift down to that place in myself that I hardly ever reach, a place far beneath my physical self, beneath my likes and dislikes, even beneath and apart from my tendency to talk too much and to look around me too sharply. And I do drift, down and away, to a place that is like the lull between dreams, or the moment of waking, when I feel like the same person I was as a child. It's a place without words, without thought—a place sweeter and deeper, even, than how I've felt lying in the arms of someone I love. I drift, without anchor, and as I float back up, underneath my surface and welling up to my surface, I feel contentment and even joy. I can feel my head nodding with pleasure. Yet I know that this joy will fade, that even the contentment will fade, and I open my eyes and look around me for something tangible to grasp or at least to touch.

I see the four walls of my kitchen, covered with Marly's drawings and the calendar landscapes, and I see the light from the kitchen falling into the next room, and Marly's sleeping and peaceful face, and I see my own table, my own hands and knees, and the bright streaks of red, blue, and silver shining on the yellow linoleum under my feet.

Aliens

I'M READING IN BED in the farmhouse I bought shortly after Marly turned twelve when I hear a car roll up the driveway. It's my ex, dropping off Marly. The car door slams, the front door opens, and Marly walks through the living room and into the kitchen and then into my room. Since I last saw her, just yesterday morning, her head has been shaved—a sixteenth-inch of brown stubble prickles over her white scalp; her soft, shoulder-length hair is gone. Though Marly is thirteen, she's still as thin as a young child. Her large, dark eyes look even more enormous than usual, and she is glaring with an intensity I've never seen coming from her. But maybe the look in her eyes, like their size, is exaggerated because of the odd new look of her head.

"You shaved your head," I say, trying to sound pleasant and offhand. Even as a baby she had not been so bald.

Marly's glaring eyes narrow before she steps out of my view, into the small bathroom adjoining my bedroom. She turns on the sink, and water rushes into the bowl.

"Who did it?" I ask.

"Maxine," Marly says over the noise of the water. Maxine is Marly's stepsister, home from college for fall break.

"It looks good on you," I say. "Not many people can shave their heads and still look good. But you've got such delicate, pretty features, and your head has a nice shape. Was it your idea, or Maxine's?"

"I don't know," Marly says. She turns off the faucets and steps back into my room, drying her small hands on the towel hanging from the door. Light from the bathroom falls across the carpet and onto the foot of my bed. Even though she is standing sideways and backlit by the light, I can see that Marly is still glaring. She rarely gets mad at me without reason, and she has never looked quite so malevolent. "Is something wrong, Marly?" I ask.

"No."

I study her disturbed yet beautiful face. "Did something happen while you were at your dad's?"

"No! Why do you always think something is wrong?"

"Because it seems like you're upset."

"I'm not upset!"

"Marly, are you sure nothing happened?"

"Nothing happened!" She takes a step toward me. "Nothing is wrong! You don't know anything! You're just a bitch!"

My body shrinks into the bed. "Marly, how can you say

that?" Until now, Marly has never called me anything worse than "mean" and "uncool."

"Because you *are*," Marly says, standing two feet from my bed and scowling down. "And all my friends think you're a bitch, too." She hesitates for a second. Then she flees from my room. I hear the accordion door creaking open from the living room onto her stairwell, her footsteps thumping up the stairs to her attic room.

I walk to my bathroom, sit on the toilet. After I pee, rather than get up, I press my face into my hands. I had thought that if I made a conscious effort, day after day, to stay on good terms with Marly as she entered and moved through her teen years, we would never grow apart. She spends every other night at her dad's, but on the nights she sleeps at my house, even though she is capable of reading whatever she wants by herself, I still read out loud to her as we lie side by side on my bed. She's grown more critical of me lately, but we never really fight.

One day a couple of weeks ago, she started lecturing me on how to behave in front of her friends so as to not embarrass her. "Why don't you just write me a list?" I said, and I handed her my journal, and she scrawled line after line:

No chewing like a cow.
No pulling your socks up way high.
No asking stupid questions.
No being nosy.
No trying to have a conversation with my friends.
No criticizing their music.
No griping at me.
No trying to be funny (it is hopeless).
No laughing when no one else is laughing.

Looking over Marly's list, I protested, "You're not letting me do anything! You might as well just write what I *can* do!" And she took the notebook back and wrote: **You can be quiet, polite, and not yourself.**

We had frowned mock-combatively at each other and then dissolved into laughter. And just yesterday, when I dropped her off at her dad's, she gave me her usual brief yet tight hug. It hadn't occurred to me that, rather than drift apart, we might experience a swift and sudden break. She has been away from me just now for only one day and one night, but in that time she seems to have moved off a million miles. It's as if spacemen have stolen my spunky yet sweet, soft-haired girl and left a bristling bald alien in her place.

I wipe the tears from my eyes and wash my face. Then I drift out into the kitchen for some cranberry juice. I lift a glass from the nearest cupboard, circle around the plant-covered sink island, pass through the patch of moonlight shining in through the skylight, and open the refrigerator. Our new kitchen is almost as large as the whole tiny apartment we moved from last year. It has plenty of room for four tables—a large oak one for eating at, a butcher block for chopping vegetables, a small table for the telephone and a medium one for plants—plus a huge stove from the fifties that sprawls along the back wall. There are four rows of cupboards, two up and two down, and everywhere you look there is another nook, cranny, or length of counter.

When Marly and I went looking for a house, she insisted I buy this one and no other: "I'm not going to live anywhere else."

"You'll have to live in whatever house I buy," I cautioned.

"But this is the best place, Mom."

"Maybe. I'm not sure I can even afford it. Why do you like it so much?"

"Because it has a big bedroom for me, and a lot of land. And I like the kids."

It was my favorite house, too, of the lowest-priced homes in the area. I closed on it a month later, and we moved in that spring.

Of the neighborhood kids near Marly's age, there are two boys down the street, a girl straight across, and a boy and a girl one street over from us. The six of them had roamed from house to house as a group all spring and summer and into the fall. But then, starting last month, only Trevor and Trish, the brother and sister living on the next street over from ours, were usually upstairs with Marly when I arrived home from work. Trish and Marly had become best friends, and Trevor and Marly were "going out." But as of last Monday, all that has changed.

As I replace the bottle of cranberry juice in the fridge, I notice that the supply of grape juice I set aside each week for the neighborhood kids is hardly touched. I open the kids' snack cupboard, and though I haven't replenished it lately, there are three bags of unopened cookies and two full bags of chips. This doesn't come as a surprise—today is Sunday, and last Monday I barred Trevor from the house. I told Marly that Trish and the other neighborhood kids were still welcome, but I haven't seen any sign of them since the incident with Trevor.

When I came home from work that day, Marly had thumped down the stairs from her room, her face pinched into a frown.

"What's the matter?" I'd asked.

"I broke up with Trevor, and then he got mad at me when I wouldn't give him back the necklace he gave me."

"Why didn't you want to give it back?"

"Because he *gave* it to me, he didn't loan it!"

"Where is it now?"

Marly had pulled it out of her pocket and held it up for me to see. The thin chain was bunched up and folded in such a way that it looked like it might be broken. Some kind of indistinct bauble, a flower or a star, was attached to one of the tiny links. I refrained from saying that it was just a cheap trinket and not worth fighting over. Instead I said, "If I were you, I'd just give it back."

"Why?"

"Because Trevor wants it back and he's mad about it."

Marly closed her hand around the necklace, gripping it in her little fist. "You're supposed to be a feminist!" she said. "You said to not let boys push me around!"

"I just don't think it's worth all the fuss."

"It is to me!" Marly said. "He only wants it back so he can give it to his new girlfriend. And I also didn't want to give it back because he was being such a dick about it. Trish and I ended up locking ourselves in the bathroom."

"In the bathroom? Why?"

"Because it's the only room in the house with a lock. Trevor was on the other side with a knife, yelling at us to come out."

"What knife?" I asked, suddenly alert, glad that Marly was the kind of child, at least so far, who told me everything.

Marly had stalked across the kitchen to the dish on the telephone table where I stash pennies and paper clips and picked up the small knife that one of my brothers gave her. It was less than three inches long, and the blade, which was folded up, was hardly more than an inch and not sharp. Still, it was a knife. "I'm going to call his parents," I said. "Trish can still come over after school, but Trevor can't be here when I'm not at home."

"Mom, he's not coming back over here, *ever*. I don't want him here *at all*."

"What happened between you two?" I asked. "Why did you break up with him?"

"Because he's a disgusting pig. He had sex with his cousin."

"What makes you think that?"

"Because he did! Trish walked in on them. She caught them lying on the couch with their pants undone."

"Well, maybe they weren't actually having sex," I said.

"Mom! What else would they be doing?"

Standing across from me, gripping the folded-up knife in her hand, Marly was stricken by a pained and knowing expression. I had taken in her suffering look and hadn't known what to say, and in the back of my mind, I'd wondered if she had dipped into my condom supply.

Holding my glass of cranberry juice, I shut the kids' snack cupboard and walk to the accordion door that closes off the stairs to Marly's room. Standing still, I listen for sounds of her. I can't hear a thing. I want to call up to her, but what would I say? *Marly, will you come down here right now so we can talk about condoms again?* Or, *Why did you come home with your head shaved and call me a bitch?* I decide it would be better to wait. Returning to the kitchen, I sit down at the big oak table and sip my juice.

A few months ago, Marly had come to me as I lay reading in bed and told me that all the other eighth graders at school were drinking alcohol and doing drugs and having sex. I'd told her that some kids probably were telling the truth, while others were just posturing. We'd talked it over, and then I'd shown Marly the ceramic canister by my bed in which I keep condoms.

I'd told her that I hoped she'd wait to have sex until she was older, but that if she didn't wait, I wanted her to use a condom every time, even the first time. It was 1994, when contracting AIDS meant certain death, and the fact that Marly could die was not an abstraction for me. I'd lost my first child, not to AIDS but to hydrocephalus when she was only two hours old, and a good friend of mine had died of AIDS the previous winter. I still remembered the cold, lifeless feel of my baby's skin and the first ugly cancer sore on my friend's handsome face. "Just take them if you think you might need them," I'd told Marly as we stared down at the creamy-white ceramic jar with a cactus flower painted on its side. "You don't have to ask permission."

After the incident last week with the necklace and the knife, I didn't look to see if any condoms were missing. I didn't know what I'd do if there had been. Probably nothing. And I hadn't wanted to spy on my daughter. But now that Marly has come home bald and glaring and acting as if something traumatic or at least unsettling has happened to her, I wonder again if perhaps she's had sex, with Trevor or someone else, and if I should do something about it.

I return to the foot of Marly's stairs and again listen for sounds of her. But I don't hear a thing—not her TV, which her dad gave her, not her radio, a present from me, not the thump of her feet on the floorboards or a creak as she turns on her bed. I set my empty juice glass in the sink and go back to my room. I eye the condom jar, on the floor in the corner near my bed, but I don't move my feet toward it.

An hour or so later, as I'm reading in bed, Marly slips in. Without apology or greeting, she stretches out across the foot of my mattress and starts telling me about her day, the cheeriness in her voice an apology of sorts, or at least an attempt to mend what's been torn. She tells me about two sisters at school who dated the same guy: first the older sister, who quickly dumped him, followed by the younger sister a week later. Then Marly tells me that her English teacher is going to bring in her pet cat, now dead and stuffed, to show to the students. "And last night, Mom," she says, "over at Dad's house, a raccoon walked up to me and almost ate right out of my hand." As Marly speaks, moving without pausing from one topic to the next, neither of us brings up our exchange of an hour ago. I want to insist, in a strong, measured voice, that she never talk like that to me again. I also want to act as if nothing has happened, invite her up beside me and open the book we are in the middle of, hold it between our close faces and read to her out loud. And I want to reach out and stroke her prickly head with my hand. Instead I spread the novel I'm reading facedown on the pillow beside me and listen, keeping quiet and still, as if my daughter is a wild animal I might inadvertently frighten off.

Marly rambles on for nearly an hour, speaking with disdain about the popular girls' clique at school, which has never welcomed her beyond its fringes, and defending a new girl she likes who wears a lot of makeup and has a wicked sense of humor, and saying how glad she is for her friend Adam—"He's spelling it A-t-o-m now, Mom"—because he is always completely nice to her. Then she sits up and says, "Don't you hate it when your armpits smell like garbage? It's amazing how much your own body can reek."

"I've never noticed you smelling bad," I say.

"That's because you're my mom. You never notice anything." She smiles, then sniffs and screws up her face and says,

"That does it—it's beyond obnoxious. I'm taking a shower."
She rolls off my bed and goes into the main bathroom, off
the kitchen, behind the door where she and Trish huddled
last week, refusing to come out or to give up the necklace. In
a little while, I hear the shower running. I scoot over to the
far side of my bed and lift the lid of the condom jar. I bought
the condoms six months ago for my own use, opened the box
and dumped the packets into the jar—a kitchen canister my
mother gave me, probably intending that I use it for sugar or
tea—but I haven't had the opportunity since then to use even
a single condom, and I haven't opened the jar since I dumped
the condoms in.

Now I stick my hand into the nest of condom packets
and stir them around, trying to count them as their foil jack-
ets whisper against each other. But it's impossible to separate
those I've already counted from those that I haven't, so I lift the
ceramic canister and tip it, and the packets slither onto my bed.

There are ten—a box of condoms, unless they've changed
the number to economize, holds a dozen. I count them again—
still ten—and then return them to the jar. As I lift the heavy
canister in my hands, I stop to look at the illustration on its
side. I noticed long ago that it was some kind of cactus flower,
but I haven't studied it closely until now.

Overlying the canister's creamy white glaze is a Venus
flytrap plant. A dozen separate, mouth-like traps grow from
the flower's central stem. Most of the traps gape with their
spiny teeth reaching outward, but four of them are closed like
cages around three moths and a bee trapped inside. Other bees
and a butterfly hover above the plant, while below them empty
traps wait, their spiny teeth reaching, their wet mouths open
and glistening. Sitting on my bed, feeling frightened, holding

the heavy canister in my hands, I wonder what has happened to Marly so far and dread what is to come.

Three years into the future, I will forbid her to date a young man who I fear might give her AIDS, since he has a reputation for having sex with many partners of both genders. One evening when Marly leaves the house to meet him, I will follow her out, trying to stop her, but she'll slip into my little Honda, which I'll have agreed to loan her before knowing her plans for the evening. She'll close the driver's door as I'm still speaking, lock it, and turn the key in the ignition. I'll shout at her to unlock the door and come back inside the house. Instead, she'll put the car in reverse and start moving backward.

I'll leap up onto the gold hood, shouting at her through the windshield to come out, forbidding her to leave the yard.

She'll back up out of the driveway with me clinging to the windshield wipers. I'll watch her silently through the windshield, the hood hard against my knees, truly at a loss as she gets the car turned around and starts driving down the road, her mouth set in a grim line, her eyes not meeting mine, her newly dyed, neon-red hair glowing in the darkness.

After a hundred feet or so, Marly will brake, and I'll jump down off the hood, and she'll drive off. When she returns home an hour later, I will ground her from using the car for a month. Yet we'll repeat a similar scenario another time, with me suffering a terrible sense of déjà vu and helplessness as the wind breaks against my back and the dark road flies past on either side and I grip the windshield wipers with my fingers like an alien who has dropped down out of the sky.

On other nights while she's still a teenager, Marly and I will take each other on other kinds of wild rides. She'll call me more ugly names, we'll shout with our faces inches apart, she'll stalk out of the house and date other dangerous boys. One night she'll dig her fingernails into my arm, and I'll slap her face. Yet she'll also continue to stretch out across the foot of my bed while she tells me about her day, and she'll tease me about what she calls my exagerrated sense of danger and my helicopter mother ways, and we'll often lie on our backs on the living room couch with our heads at opposite ends, reading separately yet together, our own books propped in our hands, our feet resting next to each other's shoulders.

But I will never read out loud to her again. We won't talk about it, we'll simply stop, in the middle of the book we had chosen, whose name I will forget. And on the night Marly comes home with her head shaved, I replace the lid on the condom jar, set it back down on the floor by my bed, and turn its illustration to the wall. Then I pick up my novel and try to read it to myself. Turning the pages, I read the words, but their meanings don't sink in. In the bathroom beyond the kitchen, the shower continues to run, hot needles of water raining down on my daughter's unprotected skin.

Fishing

SOON AFTER I BUY my house in rural Michigan, my brother Arthur, visiting from Manhattan, walks through the barn-sized garage that comes with my new property and declares it "man bait."

"What do you mean?" I ask.

"There isn't a man alive," Arthur says, turning around in the garage's vast, empty space, "who doesn't dream of a place like this for a studio or a shop."

Two years later, I'm still without a male partner, and I've rented out my garage, for the time being, to a married carpenter. "How do you expect to find a man in that backwoods, Podunk town?" Arthur admonishes over the phone. "What's the population, five hundred?"

"Including Saugatuck and Douglas," I answer, "it's around

two thousand. And Saugatuck isn't Podunk—it's a huge tourist attraction and a well-known artist colony."

"*Sheeit*," Arthur says, drawing the word out the way that black guys did in our old neighborhood in Detroit. "You are fishing for trout in a mud puddle, Annie. Ain't no single men in them towns, except for about five hundred gay boys and a couple dozen drunks. You want to catch yourself a keeper, you got to throw a wider net."

And so, after many dates and several relationships, eight years after my marriage is over, I finally take out a personal ad:

Creative, attractive, DWF, 37, 5´4˝, 120#, affectionate, assertive & physically fit. Non-smoking, laughably light drinker, casual dresser to a fault. Spiritual, politically liberal. Television IQ of a baboon. Limited social time due to my full-time job, fourteen-year-old daughter & dedication to my creative work. I like reading, writing, gardening, canoeing, x-country skiing, Lake Michigan, art & music. I'm looking for an emotionally open, articulate man for friendship, hopefully leading to an intimate relationship.

The same day my ad is printed, I check the voice mailbox I've been assigned and find the first response:

"It's Friday night and I don't have nothin' to do.... I like cuttin' down trees ... I like drivin' trucks ... Uhhhh ... I've lived in Paw Paw all my life ...Right now I'm livin' with my grammaw ... I'm forty-nine years old, but I look a whole lot younger ... Call me soon, 'cause I like to have fun."

The next responses are better, but more often than not, the men don't leave much information, and I feel funny calling someone back when all I know about him is his height, weight, age, and that he dresses casually and doesn't smoke. I almost contact a man whose introductory letter to me includes: **I** know how to cook some Greek dishes as well as Yugoslavian, German, Polish, and misguided stir fry. What IS your creative work? If nothing else, I'd like to talk with you as I feel that we've met before. (No, that's not a postal pickup line.) I really like the phrase "misguided stir fry," and I think that "postal pickup" has nice alliteration, but when he goes on to write that he owns an extensive teddy bear collection, my spike of interest takes a dive. My friend Karen urges me to respond to this man, and she scolds that I am being too rough on these guys. But there are so many responses that being picky seems not only okay, but necessary.

During my ad's third month, after I've received fifty responses and have dated three of these responders once or twice, I open a letter from a man who seems like he might be a good choice. He's included a photo in which he is standing solemnly in a field ringed by trees, looking like a model in an ad for wilderness protection. I start dating Ron and stop dating any others. Besides fields and forests, Ron likes lakes and rivers. He builds and restores wooden canoes for a hobby, and he is a freelance industrial designer for a living. He is my age, thirty-seven. He's never been married, and now he wants to get married and have children.

Although I decided long ago that I wouldn't have any more children, in some ways having another baby appeals to me deeply, and for the next three months, I consider how I might fit a baby into my life, into our lives. But after our first ninety days together, Ron announces that he wants to be with someone who is sure she wants a child, not someone who is sitting on the fence about it. He doesn't want to wait any longer to become a father. Besides, Ron says to me, crying—both of us are crying as we say good-bye for the last time—he doesn't really feel for me *in here*. He strikes his chest, a gesture that seems sincere yet makes me wonder if he took acting in high school. He likes me, Ron declares, but he doesn't love me. Strangely, since I fall in love easily, I feel the same about him. Maybe there's something to meeting someone in person and feeling a spark, having that spark set things off.

I pore back over the letters of the men who answered my ad and call several more. All three of them are a little miffed that I've taken so long to get back to them—they wrote four, five, and six months ago, and they are not happy that I've chosen them as my second-string dating roster. One of them says, "You should have answered my letter back when I sent it. You should have taken the time to politely refuse me."

I tell him that I would have had to hire a secretary to respond to everyone; he meets this remark with silence. He and my two other second choices go out with me anyway, despite their wounded pride, but only one, a devout Christian who has thrown out his TV because he's determined he is addicted to it, agrees to a second date. When I suggest a third date, he says, standing in my kitchen, throwing up his hands, "Why? We have so little in common. You eat waffles for dinner, I like burgers and steak; I'm deeply involved in my church, you think God lives in the lake. Why do you want to date me, anyway?" he finishes in exasperation.

"Well, we're both nice people," I offer.

That is the end of my personal-ad adventure. I return to dating on my own, but three years pass, and no relationship lasts. I am forty years old and have been divorced for eleven years.

My brother Arthur suggests again that I move to a larger town, or, as he puts it, "a bigger pond." But I like living where I do. I don't want to have to give up my convenient bus-driving job, even though at times I wish I could tie my passengers to the roof; I don't want to say good-bye to my good friends, not even the married ones who don't have a clue about being single; I don't want to leave Saugatuck or my beloved Lake Michigan, even though they are overrun each summer by tourists who step out into the street without looking and buzz past my head on Jet-Skis while I'm trying to swim. I pity people from Grand Rapids and Kalamazoo and other inland Michigan cities who manage to immerse themselves in The Big Lake only once or twice each summer and for the rest of the year are hemmed in by concrete and cars; I feel sorry for suburbanites from Illinois and Indiana who pass most of their lives surrounded by strip malls and lawns. I'm thrilled each time I step out my door and hear the creaky cries of sandhill cranes, I love walking down my road between fields of scrubland and corn, past maples and pines that drop down to wild marshland and then the Kalamazoo River, and I don't want to give up on finding a suitable man who resides where I feel lucky to live.

Yet all the suitable-seeming men continue to elude me. Driving back from a movie with my friend Karen late one evening, I say, "I wish I could figure out what I'm doing wrong with men. It seems that I should have been able to find one by now."

"Well, you're kind of picky," Karen responds, peering out over the steering wheel of her Ford Explorer. The night is dark, without a moon, and fog shrouds the trees on both sides of the road. "And there are more good women running around than good men. I still think you should check out the personals in the Chicago papers. Not that I want to hold Fred up as a shining example." Karen didn't meet Fred through a Chicago personal, but he lives in Chicago, and although she complains about him almost every time we talk, they've been driving back and forth to see each other for the past couple of years.

"I might end up doing that," I say. "But I'd rather find someone closer to home."

"Statistics are not in your favor."

"But all I have to do is find one. And I really think there might be something more to it than scarcity. God knows I'm not the prettiest or the nicest woman in this part of the state, but a lot of women who are uglier and meaner than me have found good guys—sometimes even great guys—to settle down with. I mean, look at Norm and Theresa. Or that terrible woman who married John Schumacher."

"You have a point," Karen says.

"It seems that I should have it figured out by now," I say again. "I really think I must be doing something wrong, or maybe a few things."

Karen brakes for a rabbit that leaps out of the fog at the road's edge. "Well, I hate to mention this because you might think I'm a flake," she says, "but have you ever thought of reading any of those self-help books? I don't know—maybe they'd have some advice you can use."

"I'm afraid I'd just be wasting my money," I say. "And I'd be too embarrassed to get them out of the library. All the people who work at the library know me."

"Well, what if I got you a book when I go to Chicago?" Karen says. "Would you read it?"

I sigh. "Sure, I'll give it a try."

Karen returns from Chicago the following weekend and presents me with three books: *If the Buddha Dated*, *Men Who Can't Love*, and *Are You the One for Me?* I read through all of *If the Buddha Dated* first, though the author irritates me by suggesting that maybe having a man in my life isn't meant to be, and that sensuous things like taking bubble baths and going swimming are suitable replacements. I set aside *Men Who Can't Love* fairly quickly, since I'm looking for a man who can. Then, with a good bit of skepticism, I pick up *Are You the One for Me?* It has a slick, cheap cover, and the title is corny, and I wonder if a black woman who has straightened every last bit of kink out of her hair and rolled the ends into Barbie-ish little flips can impart the wisdom I am seeking. But even though certain whole sentences in the text are printed in ALL CAPITAL LETTERS, what she writes makes a lot of sense. Besides reminding me of my obvious past mistakes—falling for not one but two married men—some of the advice and exercises in the book open my eyes to what I've unknowingly been doing wrong: running away from men who show a lot of interest in me, and running toward those who show ambivalence. If a man acts as if he is wholly taken with me, I think his besotted behavior foolish, so instead I've kept going out with men whose interest in me is, at best, muted.

Of course, this is making complex behaviors sound much simpler than they are. But oversimplifying helps me to see things more clearly. I realize what I need to do to turn things around: allow a man's romantic interest to come at me full tilt without running away from it. And if someone I am dating turns out to be ambivalent, then instead of trying to hold on to him, I need to let him go.

I MEET STEFAN a month after reaching these conclusions. It is a glittering day in late winter, and I am walking at the Douglas beach. The lake is frozen into two sets of icy ridges running parallel to the beach, about a hundred yards out from shore, and I'm crunching up and down these ice hills and along the tops of them, watching where I set my feet on the steeper and slippery places and walking with my gaze turned toward the horizon on the flatter, smoother stretches. Every so often I stop walking and look around me, amazed by all the beauty. The sky is blue and clear, the sun bright and dazzling, and light is shining and bouncing off the snow and ice in all directions. The open water beyond the second ridge is steely blue and calm, shifting just enough to make a soft, hissing sound as it surrounds and engulfs the small icebergs floating in it.

Only one other person is out on the ridges. All I can tell from a distance is that he is a man and that, despite the uneven, slippery ground, he is walking with his hands in his pockets. A *winter tourist*, I think. But at least he's not roaring up and down the beach on a snowmobile. He is walking back and forth along the ridges and slipping down between them, keeping a respectful distance from me.

I've quit the frozen, bumpy lake surface and am just departing for a longer walk down the shore when the man with his hands in his pockets calls out to me: "Excuse me, do you mind if I ask you a question?"

I turn to him, and he walks closer. "Hasn't that rock moved?" he asks. "Didn't that rock used to be in the water?" He points at a tall, black boulder rising from the snow-covered sand. "I'm almost sure when I came here last time, that rock was in the water, not on the beach."

I glance at the boulder and then back to the man. "A couple of years ago, it was in the water," I say. "It's not the rock that's moved, it's the water—the water has receded. We've had droughts these past few years."

"Oh, of course," the man says. He has moved close enough

to me that he doesn't have to raise his voice. He still has his hands in his pockets, and this makes me notice the relaxed slope of his broad shoulders. He is wearing a knit cap pulled down over his forehead, and he has dark hair and is wearing wire-framed glasses. His eyes are dark also, with an intelligent light in them. "Do you come here very often?" he asks.

"All the time," I answer. "I live only ten minutes away."

"Lucky you! I drove here all the way from Kalamazoo."

"I used to drive to Kalamazoo," I say. "I went to school at Western."

"So did I," the man says. "Did you graduate from there?"

"Yes I did," I answer. "Did you?"

The man says that he earned his BA from the University of Michigan and his MSW from Western. He shifts his feet on the snow-covered beach. He is wearing low-cut walking shoes that don't look warm enough.

"How did you happen to come to this beach," I ask, "if you live in Kalamazoo?" Kalamazoo is an hour away, and this beach isn't well-known. It's mainly frequented by locals and the owners of nearby cottages.

"I work in Allegan," the man says.

I squint at him, still wondering how he ended up on this beach. Allegan is also fairly far away—twenty-five miles south and east, halfway to Kalamazoo.

"I'm a therapist," the man explains, "and a couple of clients I visit at their homes live out this way. I'm not playing hooky from work. My boss thinks it's fine to take a break at the lake, as long as I'm this close. What about you—is this your home turf?"

"It is now," I say. "I came out here when I was eighteen to work at a camp just a mile up the beach from here. And then I ended up staying. But I'm originally from Detroit."

"Really?" the man says. "So am I."

"Whereabouts?" I ask, expecting the man to name one of the many suburbs that ring Detroit.

"Hamtramck," the man says.

His answer nearly makes me jump: Hamtramck shares a border with Highland Park, the city where I was raised; Detroit had grown up around these two small cities, enclosing them completely. All of Detroit's other suburbs lie outside Detroit; only our two small home cities lie within it, side by side.

Beaming, I say, "I'm from Highland Park."

"Really?" the man says. "I don't believe it! I never meet anyone from those places. I hardly ever even meet anyone who's heard of those places."

"Neither do I," I say.

We name the streets where we grew up and determine that I've never been to his street and that he has never come to mine. They are only a half mile apart but separated by Chrysler's world headquarters.

"Lost cities of our youth," the man says. "What were you doing living in Highland Park?"

"You mean, because I'm white?" I ask.

"Yeah."

"Well, my parents were big fans of Martin Luther King. What about you—what were you doing in Hamtramck?"

"My parents were second-generation racists from Eastern Europe," the man says. "But Hamtramck is not as much of a black ghetto as Highland Park is. There are still pockets of Ukrainian, Polish, and Czech holdouts who refuse to move. Whole little immigrant communities, complete with bakeries and butcher shops."

"Oh, yeah, I went to one with my mom years ago to buy Polish sausage."

"As good as you can get in Warsaw," the man says. He shifts his feet again and smiles. "Who would have thought I'd meet someone from Highland Park way out here."

"Yeah," I say, and then I can't think of what to say next. I want to get to know this man, to see him again.

"My name is Stefan Rojec," he says. He takes his hands out of his pockets. They are broad and blunt and ringless.

"I'm Annie Zito," I say, wishing it was as safe for me as it is for a man to reveal my last name to a stranger.

We stand, waiting for someone to say something or make a move.

"I should get back to work," Stefan says. "I don't punch a time clock, but I should get going anyway."

"I think I'm going to keep walking," I say.

Neither of us move, as if a string of tension held between us first needs to be snapped.

"We should talk again!" I say.

"We should!" Stefan agrees.

"Do you have a pen and a piece of paper?" I ask.

Stefan begins searching all of his pockets, and I search mine, too, but neither of us finds anything to write with or on.

"I have a pen and paper in my car," Stefan says.

"So do I," I say, regretting that I've just told him that I'm going to continue walking; now I'll feel dumb if I go up with him instead. Then I hit on an idea: "Why don't you write down your phone number and stick it under my windshield wiper?"

Stefan looks dubious.

"No, really, this will work fine," I say. "My car is the gold Honda Civic."

"What if there's another gold Honda Civic in the lot?"

"Mine's the one with a lot of rust and about ten state park stickers."

Stefan laughs. "Okay, I'll do it."

⌐

I CALL STEFAN a couple of days later, and after chatting a bit, we make tentative plans to meet for lunch at a restaurant a few miles from my house. "I can't make definite plans," Stefan says, "because of a health problem I have. It's no big deal—I'll tell you about it when I see you. But if I'm feeling under the weather, I can't just ignore it, like most people can."

"Okay," I say, thinking that it must not be AIDS, since he said it wasn't serious.

After we hang up, I think of how his voice sounded wimpy for much of our conversation—I'm not sure why, or what exactly I mean by that word. Probably it's my long-held habit of finding fault with any man who shows an interest in me. I remind myself to give him a chance, to spend our first date getting to know him rather than judging him.

Stefan is feeling fine by the weekend, and we meet at The Douglas Dinette, a large, high-ceilinged room at the end of a block of storefronts. We choose a booth under a still life of purple onions and with a view of the street, and I order a bowl of bean soup and Stefan orders a turkey burger. As we eat, he explains the health problem he mentioned: he has a congenital heart defect that has been operated on twice in his life, once when he was twelve, and the last time, a year ago. A mistake was made during the last operation—the insertion of a metal valve—and he now needs to go through another procedure to correct it.

Even though he still seems kind of "wimpy"—fastidious, or soft—I'm already starting to fall in love with him a little, this man with a wounded heart. He reminds me of Dan, my second-to-youngest brother, whose legs were amputated in an accident when he was nineteen. Always a comedian, Dan continued to crack jokes as he lay in his hospital bed in an attempt to cheer his friends and family and to let us know that he could handle it. While Stefan's attitude toward his heart is matter-of-fact rather than comic, I'm impressed that, like Dan, he doesn't seem to be trying to win sympathy through his condition. Stefan just states the facts and then moves on to another topic.

We leave the dinette and drive to Douglas Beach and walk along the icy lake. I take Stefan's ungloved hand. It is thick and short and broad, what my mom would call a peasant's hand. Stefan folds his fingers around mine, his grip strong yet relaxed, and after a stretch of silence, he tells me that he grew up in an extremely dysfunctional family, with an alcoholic father who beat his mother. I ask Stefan if his father was also abusive to him and his siblings, and Stefan says with a bitter edge, "Yes, but not too often. Only when we got in his way. He didn't chase us down, like he did our mother." Stefan then reveals that he is a recovering alcoholic who attends AA regularly and hasn't had a drink in fifteen years. Upon hearing this, my admiration for him grows. My brother Arthur quit using alcohol and other drugs more than a decade ago, and I'm proud that he's stayed off them. And it always impresses me when a person overcomes a strong addiction, especially when he's also had to rise above a dismal childhood.

Stefan drives back to my house with me, and we sit on my couch and continue to talk. Then I present him with a published copy of my story collection. I feel guilty for giving my book to a near-stranger when I've sold copies to good friends, but my gift has the desired effect.

"Wow," Stefan says. He runs his hand over the red and silver dust jacket, the crisp black lettering. "This is a real book. By you. I'm impressed."

At my door, I hug him good-bye, and he says, "I like the ways you touch me."

I look at him, pleased but slightly puzzled.

"Your hug just now," he says, "and when you took my hand on the beach."

"Oh," I say. "Well, good. I liked touching you." I look down at the rug, feeling foolish. Probably he learned to talk that way in therapy, of which he had a lot, he said during our walk, before becoming a therapist himself.

For our next date, Stefan invites me to his apartment at the edge of Kalamazoo. He lives in a condo complex with a small, man-made lake and a channel-like river cut through its center and wooded trails that wind all through the grounds. As we stroll under the leafless trees, Stefan tells me without prompting that he has never been married and that lately he's been thinking that he wants to get married and settle down. He is forty-eight years old, he says, and it seems that if he doesn't do it now, it might not ever happen. We pass a restaurant on the condo grounds, and then a gym and a huge, glassed-in swimming pool, in which I imagine myself swimming laps, the sun shining in through the floor-to-ceiling windows and lighting up the water. Stefan doesn't mention me joining him in the pool, but he says we can take out a canoe when the weather warms up.

After we return to his apartment, Stefan sits down right in the middle of his small couch, and I sit down to the left of him. The couch is so short—nearly a love seat—that with him sitting on the middle of it, the side of my leg almost brushes his. As we talk about this and that, I rub his back with my hand. We talk some more, and I put my arm around his shoulders. He continues to talk, and I lean in close and nuzzle his cheek.

"Stop doing that!" he says.

I sit up straight and look at him, startled.

"You're making an assumption!"

I move a little away from him; I can't move too far, because the arm of the short couch is right at my left elbow.

"If a man came on strong like that, he would be considered out of line. Well, the same should hold true for women."

"I'm sorry," I say. "I didn't think you'd mind."

He is staring angrily at the floor. He also looks embarrassed, perhaps by his own outburst. His face has flushed bright red.

"At the end of our last date," I say, "you said you liked the ways I touched you."

"Well, now you're moving too fast."

I am too confused and startled to speak. I see that I should have noticed that my touches were making him uncomfortable, yet if he wanted me to keep my distance, then why did he sit down on the middle of the short couch, rather than off to one side? Maybe he expected me to take a seat on the overstuffed chair across the room.

"When I started dating my last girlfriend," Stefan says, "we agreed that it was just a temporary arrangement. She was in love with some other guy, but he wasn't in love with her, so we decided to have a relationship that was purely sexual. But then, after seven months, she decided that she loved me after all, and that what we had was the real thing. And I didn't have any say in it! Suddenly I'm in the midst of this relationship that has turned into something more than what we said. I don't want that to happen again. This time, I want a vote!"

The idea of voting on a relationship strikes me as funny, but I'm too surprised and dismayed to laugh. I sit pressed up against the arm of the little couch, wondering how we've reached this impasse, and remember a remark made by my brother Arthur: that when it comes to romance and sex, men like to think it's their idea. I grip my hands in my lap. I am terrible at playing hard to get, and it doesn't seem fair to have to. And if I have to play by sexist rules to get a man, will I end up in a sexist relationship?

We go for another walk before I leave, and Stefan puts his hand on my arm just as we reach the apex of a tiny, arched bridge that is artificially cute—a simple, straightforward plank arrangement would look nicer. "I'm sorry if I hurt your feelings," he says, looking into my eyes and seeking out the sorrow lurking there as if it's a kind of sustenance, sucking the hurt from my eyes with his gaze as if it's marrow from a bone and he finds it tasty. Then he kisses me. Maybe he likes to wound women, after seeing his father do it so often. But maybe I've just scared him, by coming on too strong. Maybe things will work out all right after all.

⌒

STEFAN CANCELS OUR next couple of dates, claiming that he isn't feeling well. He can't afford to get sick, he says, because if he does, his doctor will postpone the heart procedure, and he needs the procedure to get well; plus, he's already bought his plane ticket to Boston, where the operation is scheduled. I also cancel several dates because I think I'm coming down with a sore throat, and I don't want to infect him. Three times, I make cakes for Stefan's birthday, then feel sick and put the cakes in the freezer. I make six cake rounds in all, of which I eat one and freeze five. I just celebrated my own birthday, in March, and several of my women friends gave me flowers, including a pot of miniature narcissi called tête-à-tête, or face-to-face, because two blooms sprout from each single stem, so close to each other that they touch. The way things are going, I think, I'll never get face-to-face again with Stefan.

For twelve days, my throat remains thick and irritated with the beginnings of a sore throat that never arrives. Finally, I figure out that I'm just reacting to a seasonal allergy and, two days later, dosed with an antihistamine and feeling fine, I visit Stefan, bringing a belated birthday cake that I've pulled from the freezer. This is only our third date. We've talked on the phone but haven't seen each other in three weeks. Stefan is preparing a pork roast and potatoes and salad for our dinner, and he seems relaxed and happy to see me—perhaps all that absence has made his heart grow fonder. After he has ushered me into the kitchen and poured me a glass of grape juice, he says, "By the way, I liked your novel."

I correct him, in my head: *it's a collection of stories*. Most take place in Detroit, and Stefan tells me it was fun to vicariously revisit his old stomping grounds. "And you're a good writer," he says. "I was already familiar with the setting, but I felt at home with the characters, too. The girl, especially. And her brothers." I tell him thanks, feeling pleased.

We are standing in the kitchen during a pause in the dinner preparations when I notice a strange noise: a scratchy, mechanical ticking that resounds clearly in the tiny room. I lift my head and listen, trying to figure out what I'm hearing.

"You're noticing it, aren't you," Stefan says. "It's my heart."

"Oh," I say. It sounds like the metal workings of a ticking clock. Like Captain Hook, I think. No, not Hook, but the crocodile.

"That's the mechanical valve, opening and closing. It bothered me at first, but then I got used to it. It's a small price to pay for what it does."

"It reminds me of my furnace," I say. "The blower is really loud, and the sound used to annoy me. But then my furnace broke down, and once it was fixed, I was glad to hear the blower, because it meant the furnace was working and I'd stay warm."

"Exactly," Stefan says. His heart scrapes and ticks. "It's only noticeable at odd moments. And only when my surroundings are completely silent. Like when the refrigerator motor turns off."

I nod and smile. His heart continues to tick. "Let me put on some music," Stefan says, and he steps into the living room and turns on the classical station.

After dinner, sitting on the couch with the radio still playing, Stefan slips an arm around my shoulders. "Is this okay?" he asks.

"Sure."

I let him continue to take the lead. Slowly, gently, he puts his other arm around me, and then we are kissing.

"How are you doing?" he asks.

"Fine."

"You're a good kisser," he says. We kiss some more. He doesn't take it any further, and neither do I. When I last talked to my brother Arthur, he said, falling back on his store of fishing metaphors, that Stefan, being forty-eight and never married, is like a big old, sly fish, and they are the hardest to catch. "He's been slipping the bait off the hook for so many years," Arthur said, "that he's gotten really good at it. And if you try to pull back on that hook too soon, you won't catch him, you'll scare him off."

But I'm not sure that I want to hook a man; what I want, rather, is one who will swim along beside me.

⌒

STEFAN'S HEART PROCEDURE goes fine, and after he's been home for a few days and is feeling well enough for company, I bring him a big pot of clam chowder. He is pleased by the good food and thanks me a few times. He says he is tired, so I leave early. He closes the door behind me without having touched me. It seems to me that if he were not feeling so ambivalent, he would at least have held my hand.

When we next speak on the phone, Stefan tells me that he doesn't want to see me the coming weekend. "I need things to go more slowly," he says.

I think of how I decided, after reading the relationship books my friend Karen gave me, to stop treading softly around men, to stop waiting around for their ambivalence to flower into love. Maybe it's time to find out if it's time to move on. "Is it really that you want to go slowly," I say, "or is it that you don't want to be in a relationship with me at all?"

He gives a sigh. "I don't know if I want to be in a relationship with you or not," he says. "I need more data."

"More *data*?"

"Sorry for sounding clinical," he says. "I would like to see you again, but not for two or three weeks."

I feel my heart let down; once again, I am involved with a man who wants less from me than I do from him. "If you don't want to date me at all," I say, "that's okay. But I'd rather know."

"I still want to date you," Stefan says. "Just not steady dating yet. I've been so involved with my health lately that I don't have a lot of energy left over for a relationship."

"Okay," I say. "Do you want to make a plan for two weeks from now, or do you want to wait and see?"

"I'd rather wait," he says.

I'm angry after I hang up, but then I think maybe I'm being unfair, that I should give him more of a chance. He has been understandably preoccupied with his health lately, and why should I expect his interest in me to develop as quickly as mine always does?

I call my friend Sarah in Massachusetts and bring her up to date on my dating life, and she sighs and says, "He sounds like me—how I stick my toe into a relationship and then pull it back out. I just freeze up. Maybe that's what happens when you've lived with an abusive person, whether it's your father or your husband."

My daughter, who is eighteen and never without a boyfriend for more than a few days, has a different response: "I think if a guy isn't wild about you right from the first, you should dump him."

"It can be more complicated than that," I answer. "Sometimes people have been through a lot. It's not just a matter of baggage—people can be as wounded as if they've been through a war."

"Well, then maybe," Marly says, "you should find a man who ran off to Canada instead of getting blasted half to death."

I smile into the phone; Marly has been verbally quick from the moment she learned to speak. Still, I want her to see my side of this. "So, if someone has been damaged or had a rough life, are you saying I should write him off?" I'm thinking of my brother Dan and his crushed and severed legs, and also of my brother Arthur, who for the past decade has suffered from seizures that have grown progressively worse.

"He can be damaged," Marly concedes, "as long as he still thinks you're really hot."

⌒

ALL WEEK, AND INTO the next week, I refrain from calling Stefan—in the past, I would have come up with some rationalization for calling and picked up the phone and punched the numbers. "Take your time, take it slow," my brother Arthur counsels when I call him. "Keep the bait on the hook, but don't hit him in the face with it. Sooner or later, even an old, battle-scarred fish will swim up close."

Meanwhile, I'm waking at seven instead of at eight in the mornings and getting more writing than usual done before I have to stop at noon for my job, plus I have my evenings free to read. It makes me want to reconsider this whole man-mate idea. But I can't deny my desire for a companion of my own to turn to, which at times I feel so keenly; it's a need that can't be met by just my friends and family. When my women friends go home to their husbands, when my parents turn to each other, when my brothers pair off with their wives, I feel like the cheese in that children's song, standing all alone. Sometimes I find myself singing lines from the song in my head:

> *The farmer takes a wife*
> *The farmer takes a wife*
> *Hi-ho the derry-o*
> *The farmer takes a wife...*
> *The cheese stands alone*

The cheese stands alone
Hi-ho the derry-o
The cheese stands alone.

At least the cheese—small comfort—is standing rather than prostrate. It occurs to me that Stefan and I both are like lone hunks of cheese.

A few days before the two weeks have passed, Stefan calls and invites me to his place for dinner. I'm surprised as well as pleased to hear from him. "Should I bring some artichokes?" I ask. During one of our conversations, it came up that he has eaten artichoke hearts from a jar, but he has never eaten a fresh, whole artichoke.

"Sure," he says. "What do they go with?"

"Pretty much anything. They're a vegetable."

"Well, I know that. But I have no idea how to cook them or eat them."

"I'll show you."

When I walk into Stefan's apartment, it feels warm and cozy and the air is fragrant and spicy. He has made a meatloaf with twice-baked potatoes—one of my ex-mother-in-law's specialties, I can't help noting, but I don't tell Stefan this. As the potatoes continue to bake, I steam two artichokes. Then we bring everything to the table and sit down. Stefan looks around at all the food with a soft, fond gaze. He forks a piece of the meatloaf into his mouth and closes his eyes halfway. As he softly, slowly chews, pressing the meat with his teeth, a dreamy look comes over his face.

"It's fun to watch you eat," I say. "You always look so contented."

"I do?"

"Yes. You look as if you're completely at peace."

He laughs. "Well, I do like to eat. Perhaps too well." He glances down at his belly, which is slightly rounded. Above his belly, his chest rises broad and muscled. In addition to swimming daily laps in the condo pool, he lifts weights twice a week in the gym.

"Every time I've seen you eat," I say, "you're like that—just utterly pleased."

"Stop it—you're going to make me self-conscious. And I haven't even started on my artichoke yet. When are you going to show me?"

"There's nothing to it," I say. "A three-year-old can do it." I pluck a leaf from the artichoke nearest me, dip its thickened base into a little bowl of lemon juice mixed with butter, turn the leaf over, and scrape the meat from the base with my lower teeth.

"How did the first person ever figure that out?" Stefan asks.

"They must have been trying everything," I say. "I've never seen one of these growing, or even a picture, but I've heard that they grow fairly tall, and this part that we're eating, it's the bud of a flower. So these things that we call leaves, really they are petals."

Stefan hasn't yet plucked a petal. "Aren't you going to try it?" I ask. "Do you want me to stop watching you?"

He smiles. "There is something about your gaze," he says. "It's very intense. But no, you can watch." He plucks a petal or leaf, turns it over and squints at its meaty end, then dips the end into the sauce and scrapes it over his teeth. A distant but thoughtful expression grows on his face. A faint smile blossoms. It occurs to me that his smiles always look a little sad. "I like it," he says. He plucks another leaf and dips and scrapes the meat from it. "The teachable moment," he says.

I've never heard that expression before, and this must register on my face.

"Do you know what that means?" he asks.

I shake my head.

"Well, there's a window when it's possible for a thing to be learned. For instance, children can learn to speak any language without an accent, but adults can't acquire accentless speech. And there are certain things that can't be learned at all, the avenues for learning them have closed." He smiles again. "I'm glad I haven't passed the teachable moment for eating artichokes. They're very good."

After dinner, with the radio on, we sit on the couch and kiss. Again, I let Stefan take the lead, although I have mixed feelings about acting passive. But at least he is leading instead of backing off. I want to ask him how the data collection is coming, but I don't want to scare him off or ruin the moment. Still, thoughts related to "data" keep running through my head, making me smile to myself. *Have you collected enough data now? How about now? After you gather all the data you need, do you plan to run experiments?* After a while, Stefan says, "Do you want to move to my bedroom?" I say yes, and he takes my hand and leads me there. It's a small room, almost filled by the dresser and the high double bed.

"Can I take off your shirt?" Stefan asks.

I pause. "Okay," I say.

I let Stefan pull my long-sleeved shirt over my head. As usual, I'm not wearing a bra, and the air on my nipples feels—well, *nippy*. Stefan keeps his shirt on. We lie down on the bed and continue to kiss. "Can I take off your socks?" Stefan asks.

I laugh. It seems that a woman who says yes to baring her

breasts wouldn't balk when it comes to revealing her feet, but I don't remark on this. "Sure," I say.

Stefan scrunches down at the end of the bed and removes my socks. He doesn't seem fastidious to me anymore, just gentle and soft in a sweet way, although he also seems to have an underlying, harder edge. We kiss and make out some more. Stefan turns off the light, without asking me about it first. Then he takes off his own shirt in the dark. I can feel several thick, raised scars on his arms and on his chest, running over and below his heart. I can't hear Stefan's heart ticking, maybe because my own heart is beating hard. We make out some more, and Stefan asks me if he can remove my pants.

I hesitate. "Yes," I say. "But I think I'll leave my underwear on for now."

We make out stripped to our underwear. We are both breathing heavily. "Do you want to have sex?" Stefan asks.

"Maybe," I say. "If you have a condom."

Stefan leans up on one elbow in the dark, causing the bed to creak. "First I need to ask something," he says. "What does sex mean to you?"

"What do you mean?" I ask.

"I mean, how much emotional weight does it carry for you? When you have sex with someone, does it make you more emotionally attached?"

"Yes."

"That could be a problem," Stefan says.

I don't like where this conversation is heading, but it's better than having sex with a man who keeps his thoughts to himself and then doesn't call me again or return my calls to him, something that happened to me shortly after my divorce. It's better to get things out into the open. "Getting close has been a problem for me in the past," I say. "That's why I stopped having sex with every boyfriend. I was having too many relationships that lasted just a few months, or a year or so, and having had sex made breaking up harder." Also—although I don't tell Stefan this—I feel that my list of sexual partners is getting too long. There were three between the ages of fifteen and eighteen, then just one, my boyfriend, Ray, who became my husband, between the ages of eighteen and twenty-nine, then five more in the first eight years after my divorce. If I keep this up, my list will be incredibly long by the time I reach my eighties.

"I guess we'd better not have sex then, if you aren't able to view it casually."

"Probably not," I say.

We continue to make out. "Or maybe," I say, stroking the soft skin of his muscled shoulders, "we should just have it anyway."

He pulls back from me and looks into my eyes, holding me gently by the elbows. I can barely see him in the dark. "I don't think that's a good idea," he says.

We cool down, stroking each other casually. After awhile, we sit up and collect our clothes. Stefan hands me my shirt. Then, sitting at the end of the bed, he carefully and gently pulls my socks onto my feet. He pulls on his own socks next, his face thoughtful and a little sad.

ON THE PHONE during the week, we make plans to have dinner again on the coming Friday, which happens to be Good Friday. We chat some more, and then Stefan suggests that we get together for Easter dinner. I think he means that he wants to get together on Sunday instead of, rather than in addition to, Friday, and after a bit of confused talk he says, "Oh. I see why you thought that. Because I said I didn't want to get together too often."

"Yeah," I agree. "You said once every couple of weeks."

"And now I'm suggesting twice in one weekend."

"Yes."

"Well, I meant both times, if that's okay with you."

"Sure," I say, pleased.

We go out for dinner on Friday in Kalamazoo, and then we return to Stefan's condo. Again, Stefan asks me if he can remove my shirt and my socks, and he takes off his shirt only after he's turned off the lights. I suppose that he doesn't want me to see his scars, even though I can feel them against my skin, rising from his arms and chest in hard ridges.

I don't reveal my own scars, which Stefan will see only if we strip ourselves further: the dark, horizontal line at the top of my pubic hair from which first Sophie, who quickly died, and, a year later, healthy Marly were pulled from my body; plus an array of faint stretch marks, very low on my belly—iridescent, blue-white flaws that shimmer like minnows. I'm so used to my twice-healed C-section scar that I rarely think about it, and the stretch lines are subtle, and even, I think, kind of pretty. But I don't see any reason to pull down the elastic of my panties and point out the marks left by my babies, and I don't want to fully undress with Stefan unless we are going to be fully sexual.

ON EASTER SUNDAY, Stefan is even more pleased than Marly is that I've made them each an Easter basket, with dyed eggs and jelly beans and chocolate eggs and a chocolate rabbit. "I've never had an Easter basket before," Stefan says, and I wonder what else he has missed out on or been subjected to as a child, besides no Easter baskets and his father beating his mother.

After Stefan leaves, I ask Marly what she thinks of him. "He's dorky, Mom," she says. "And kind of boring. And that haircut is god-awful!"

"You always find fault with my boyfriends," I complain.

"I don't see how you can go out in public with a man who wears a mullet."

"It's not a mullet. He just has a few wispy pieces of hair in the back."

"That's a mullet, Mom. And a bald guy with a mullet— that's as bad as you can get."

"Well, usually, I don't like hair that's cut like that. But I think it looks good on him. Kind of sporty."

"You're cracked. And even without the haircut, the man is a dork."

"What does that mean? That a guy is intelligent, but not cool? So what? At our age, being cool is no longer important."

"Plus he walks like a duck," Marly says.

I had noticed this, too. "There are worse things than walking like a duck," I say.

I drive to Stefan's house the following weekend, and we again eat dinner and make out on his bed but don't have sex. As before, Stefan turns off the light prior to removing his shirt, but this time the room is gray rather than black, and I can see the scars crossing his arms and his chest, shining white. I want to trace them with my hands; I want to mention their presence, allow them into full light. But I'm sure Stefan will retreat at any acknowledgment or mention, so I act as if I can't feel them or see them.

SEVERAL WEEKS PASS, during which Stefan and I talk on the phone. It's my turn to have him over to my house, but he keeps rebuffing my invitations. Memorial Day weekend is approaching. Stefan says he'd like to spend it with friends in Muskegon, an hour up the coast from Saugatuck, and that maybe he'll stop to see me on his way home. "But maybe not," he says. "I'd rather leave it up in the air."

Of course you would, I say to myself. *Just like you leave everything else. So high up that you never have to come down.* But all I say out loud is, "Okay," trying to hide my irritation and disappointment.

"I'll call you from their house if I'm going to come," he says. "But don't wait for me. I don't expect you to sit at home, waiting for my call."

I do stay at home for most of that Sunday, trying to make sense of the rough draft of a new story I am writing, feeling fairly sure that I'm wasting my time, with the story and with Stefan. I leave the house only for a walk. Stefan doesn't call that day, and he doesn't call on Monday, either, or on Tuesday, by which time he is back home in Kalamazoo. Okay, I say to myself. *This is the point where I usually come up with a rationalization for calling the guy, but this time, I'm not going to do that.* When I think of calling him the following Friday, I tell myself, *This is the same bad pattern of trying to hold on to a man whose feelings for me are ambivalent at best.* Maybe he is past the teachable moment for being in a serious relationship. I hope I'm not past the teachable moment of knowing when it's time to quit.

He doesn't call me for six weeks, and I don't call him. Occasionally, I think, *What if his heart has malfunctioned? What if he's been in an accident?* But I know in my own heart that he is almost surely fine. I imagine him puttering in his garden, swimming laps in the pool, attending AA meetings, perhaps dating someone new.

Finally, wanting closure, I call him after six weeks have passed.

"Oh, hi, how are you?" he asks in a high voice.

"Pretty good," I say. "How are you?"

"I'm doing well," he says. "I'm sorry I never called you."

"That's okay," I say. "I figured you didn't call me because you weren't interested in dating me anymore, but I just wanted to make sure that nothing had happened."

"Like with my heart, you mean?"

"Yeah, or an accident or something."

"No, nothing has happened," he says.

"That's what I figured," I say.

"You were just going too fast for me," he says.

I think of a big old, slow fish, nibbling on the bait, then backing off. In the past, I would have said, "Well then, maybe we can go more slowly—how would you like to proceed?" But now I say, "I just wanted to know for sure, rather than wondering. I just wanted a more solid ending."

"That's understandable," Stefan says.

"Okay, well, good luck," I say.

"Good luck to you, too," Stefan says.

I'm irritated as I hang up the phone. *What a loser!* And to think he makes his living advising others about their personal lives! I come up with a couple more nasty words to call him— *wimpy* and *soft*—but then I remember his lousy childhood and his sad smile, and my anger vanishes. Mostly, I am proud of myself for not dragging this out, for not chasing after someone who does not wish to be caught. But I still feel a little sad as I watch him swim off, his scarred skin shining faintly, like the scales of a carp, his slow-moving body disappearing so quickly it is as if he had never come near me.

Strays

ONE SPRING EVENING as I'm reading in bed, Marly calls and tells me that there is a man sleeping on her porch. "I think he's *moved in*, Mom. The couch on the porch is his new home base. He's planning to *stay*."

"How long has he been there?"

"Three nights and three days. He's wandered off a few times, but he keeps coming back."

"Where did he come from?"

"I don't know. Most likely the shelter or the rehab place. Or maybe he used to live at the liquor store."

The homeless shelter, the rehab center, and the liquor store are all located near Madison Manor, a Victorian mansion in Grand Rapids whose three stories and carriage house have been carved up into sixteen apartments. Marly has the first floor apartment on the right and in the front—two small rooms plus a tiny kitchen; high ceilings with carved wooden moldings; three tall bay windows that look out onto the wide, rickety porch. All that lies between the liquor store and the manor's porch is an alley and a parking lot, and the rehab center and the homeless shelter are just a few doors down the street. Because of this proximity, it isn't rare for homeless or at least wandering, lost men to stumble around and even upon Madison Manor.

Marly has related a few of these incidents to me. There was the morning not long after she moved in when she was sitting out on the porch drinking a smoothie straight from the blender jar. Suddenly a man rose up from the bushes, fumbling with his zipper. *Oh no, he's going to flash me,* Marly thought, *and I'm going to have to hit him with this blender.* But the man's hands drifted from his fly, and he stumbled away. He hadn't come to flash anyone but only to urinate in the bushes. Another time a man stumbled into those same bushes and passed out. Marly figured drinking was most likely the cause, but she wasn't sure; the man could have had a heart attack. She dialed 9-1-1, and, a half hour later, the police showed up, shook the man awake, and led him away. The worst time was when a drunken man walked up onto the porch and then strode back and forth, talking loudly. Marly asked him to leave, and he shouted at her, "I'm an American Indian. This is my land. Get off my fucking land!" Marly shouted back, "Yeah, well I'm paying rent for this fucking porch, so you're the one who better get off it." Then she went inside, feeling shaken. Later she told me, "He looked like he *was* an Indian, Mom. And what he said made some sense. But what was I supposed to do? Go back to fucking Europe?"

Now Marly says, "But I'm not really calling about the guy living on the porch. I'm calling to see if you can come up to

Grand Rapids for dinner tomorrow, rather than me coming down there. I have a paper I need to finish, and that will save me some time."

"Sure," I say. "Do you want to go out to that Chinese place?" There's a Chinese diner we like just around the corner, across the street from the liquor store.

"Yes. I don't even feel like eating at home with that guy right outside."

"Has he done anything threatening?"

"No. He's invited me to come out and share a bottle of wine, is all."

I don't have to ask to know that Marly declined. If she liked wine, she might have joined the man on the couch without first thinking it through. But the only liquor she ever drinks is Kahlua with cream.

"How did the guy happen to choose your particular porch for camping out?" I ask.

"Well," Marly says, "it's partly my fault. I was sitting out on the picnic table on the porch with a bunch of my apartment mates a few nights ago, and the homeless man was sleeping across the porch from us, on the couch. It was a cold night, even though it's spring, and there was this blanket—a really nice, warm comforter—in the lobby that someone left there when they moved out. I didn't really think about the ramifications. I just thought that the guy must be really cold sleeping there without a blanket, and that here was a comforter no one was using, and so I got up and fetched it and covered him up. He opened his eyes and said, 'Thanks, honey.' And he's been there, pretty much, ever since. I didn't think of it when I covered him up, but the couch is right outside my living room windows—I mean *right* outside. I don't feel like I can even open my window, let alone my curtains with him there. And my curtains don't quite close all the way—there's a gap."

"Why was he sleeping on the couch in the first place?" I ask.

"I don't know. I guess because it was empty and he was tired."

⌒

THE DAY AFTER Marly tells me about the homeless man sleeping on her porch, I drive up to Grand Rapids and see him for myself. It's only six in the evening with plenty of daylight left, yet he is sound asleep, his head tucked under one arm, the thick, soft comforter wrapped around his long, skinny body. He's a black man, I notice, from the texture of his hair and the light-brown skin of his exposed hand, which is curled up like a child's.

Marly buzzes me into the lobby, furnished with second-hand chairs and couches and dominated by a grand wooden staircase leading to the upper floors, and then she unlocks the door to her apartment, leaning down to prevent the younger of her two cats from running out past her feet.

"Your homeless guy is asleep," I say.

"That's all he does is sleep," Marly says, her neon-red hair glowing in the lobby's dimness. "Or else drink and stare out at the street. Except once I opened the curtains, and he was looking into my living room. And another time I walked up toward the front windows without opening the curtains, and I'm pretty sure I saw him there again, sitting up on the couch and looking in."

"That's a little scary," I say.

"I know. I've stopped walking up to the curtains, because it was freaky to see his face there, staring right at me. So, since

I'm not checking up on him, who knows how often he's doing it. I asked Mitch to ask him to leave, and Mitch said he did, but it obviously hasn't done any good."

"Where's Mitch now?" I ask.

"He's here—in the bedroom. He's about to go out."

I'm glad that Mitch, who lives with Marly, isn't coming to dinner with us. He seems to me not many steps above the homeless man. Jobless, he had been living temporarily with friends when he met Marly. At first he continued to spend his nights at the apartments of various friends, but then gradually he started living with Marly exclusively. It was impossible to tell exactly when that had happened, because he didn't have many belongings other than a few clothes.

Sometimes Marly seems to enjoy Mitch's company, and other times, to tolerate it. She says that they don't have an exclusive relationship. Considering that so far I've had sex with eight more men than my mother, who has only ever made love with her husband of nearly fifty years, I don't feel that I should or can say much to Marly about her sex life, unless I think her safety is being threatened. But sometimes when she mentions another guy, I will ask, "Is he a friend or a boyfriend?" She has a lot of answers to that question: "Just a friend." "Some of each." "It depends." "Oh, Mom, why do you always have to have a category?"

While Marly rummages in a drawer for her extra set of keys, Mitch comes out of the bedroom, wearing his usual grubby jeans and a gray T-shirt with a band logo on it. "Hi, Mom," he says to me.

"Hi, Mitch," I answer, trying to smile rather than grimace. He started calling me Mom the first time he met me. It threw me off balance—I couldn't tell if he was joking. And everything about him makes me uneasy—his smile is oily, his eyes seem insincere, and during the months he doesn't have a job, which is more months than not, he lives off Marly's meager wages and the money her dad and I give her for college.

"You and Marly going out to dinner?" Mitch asks.

"Yes," I say. With any of Marly's other friends and boy-friends, I would add, "Want to come with us?" I've taken Mitch out just once. He spent the entire dinner calling Marly affectionate names and telling her he loved her. Marly responded as if faintly charmed, yet as if trying to hide from herself that something was off kilter.

"Well, I'm going out with a buddy of mine," Mitch says, slipping on his motorcycle jacket. He had to sell his bike, Marly told me, but he's held on to his jacket and his helmet.

"Okay," I say. "Have fun."

"I will." Mitch's lips stretch up tightly at the corners, and then he strolls over to Marly, tips up her chin with his hand, and kisses her on the lips. "I love you, darlin'," he says.

Marly smiles appreciatively rather than answer in kind. "What time will you be back?" she asks.

"I'm not sure," Mitch says. "I haven't seen this buddy in a long time. Mind if I take the car?" He is referring to my little gold Honda, which I gave Marly so that she could safely travel to work and school. Marly murmurs that he can use the car, and Mitch glances back at me. "Bye, Mom." He smiles again, with his face in the doorway. Then he pulls the door closed behind him, and I let out my breath.

Marly ties on her Converse All Stars and then, searching for her purse, paces around her apartment. It is a grand old faded place, with all kinds of nooks and odd angles, and still charming even though the floors have been covered in cheap brown carpeting. The high, cracked walls have been painted an elegant, creamy white, and the three bay windows that face out onto the porch are taller than a tall man, while the ill-fitting curtains that don't quite cover them are cheap and modern.

Marly finds her purse on the floor by the couch and then points at the front of her apartment where the heavy drapes are drawn. "See the gap?" she says. There is a two-inch-wide space at the center where the two halves fail to meet. "The guy on the couch was looking in through there."

"I can ask him to leave on our way out to dinner," I offer.

"No, don't," Marly says quickly. "I don't know how he'll react. He might start shouting like that Indian man."

We leave for the restaurant. As we step out onto the porch, the homeless man sits up. "Hi, Beautiful!" he sings out to Marly. His mouth breaks into a sunny, gap-toothed smile. Then he catches sight of me, beyond Marly. "Oh!" he says. "You must be her mom. Now I see where she gets being gorgeous from!" He grins at me, and, before I can think, I smile back. I can't remember the last time anyone has implied that I might be beautiful. My last, reluctant dating partner, whom I've come to think of as the cold fish, never complimented my appearance, and even when my earlier dates and boyfriends mentioned my looks, the words they used were "attractive" and "cute." Because of my recent dissatisfying dating experience, I've decided to steer clear of men for a while; and yet here I am lighting up at a few warm and flattering words from a drunken homeless man who has taken up occupancy outside my daughter's window. After my brief, inadvertent smile, I break eye contact with the man. But both Marly and I say "Hi" as we hurry down the steps.

We walk to the corner and cross, avoiding the liquor store's front entrance, and duck with relief into the little

Chinese restaurant where the owners and employees are not conversant in English. We order our food by checking off items on a paper menu and turn the menu in, and, as we sit at a table to wait, I envision Marly getting up from the picnic table on the manor's porch, walking into the manor's lobby, returning with the blanket, unfolding it, and gently draping it over the sleeping man. She might have done this even if she had considered the ramifications. All her life, she's had a tender heart for strays.

The first were Uno and Dos, baby bunnies she and the neighborhood kids found whose nest had been destroyed by a dog. All six of the neighborhood kids took turns feeding the bunnies with an eyedropper, keeping them in a cardboard box that they moved from house to house. Uno died on the second day, but Dos lived long enough to be released. Marly also tended a string of stray cats that had hung around outside our door, putting out food and water, and a blanket, too, stuffed into a plastic bin. And then there was the baby possum.

I found it while taking a walk one afternoon before work. I came across its dead mother first, hit by a car, on the road near my house that winds by the Kalamazoo River. On my way back, returning along the same stretch of road, I saw that the dead possum had been flipped over—perhaps hit by another car—so that its belly was exposed. Also exposed, lying a foot from its mother, was a tiny, hairless, dead baby. And on the mother possum's belly, clinging to a nipple, was a second hairless baby, squirming and sucking ferociously on its dead mother's teat.

I considered taking the live baby home and caring for it. I considered pulling it from its mother and breaking a path through the undergrowth and drowning the pitiful little creature in the river. And I considered letting nature take its course. Possums have never been my favorite animals, and I've liked them even less ever since I rolled my car while trying to avoid one that charged my front tire like a kamikaze. As the tiny pink possum noisily sucked, I looked down at it and its dead mother and sibling, debating to myself. Then I returned to my car and drove to my afternoon shift.

Marly, who was sixteen then, stopped by my work in her dad's car, which she had borrowed for the afternoon. As we sat and chatted in the break room, I told her about the possums I'd found. Her eyes had widened in astonishment and horror.

"The one baby was still *alive*?" she asked.

"Yes."

"And you just *left* it there?"

"I thought of taking it with me, but I decided to let nature take its course."

"A car running over a baby's mother isn't *nature*, Mom."

I opened my mouth to say something, but I didn't really have an answer, so I just pulled in my breath and let it out.

"If *my* mother were run over and I was a baby, would you just *leave me there*?"

"No, but you're not a possum."

Marly gave me a dirty look and rose from her chair. "I can't believe you just walked away. Where exactly was it?" She pulled her car keys from her purse.

"Are you going to go look for it?"

"Yes!" she said, as if I'd asked a stupid question.

"It's down by the river, where I always walk. Right after the first open stretch."

"And how long ago was it?"

I looked at my watch. "About an hour and a half."

"Okay," she said, more to herself than to me, sounding determined.

When I got home from work that evening, Marly was holding the baby possum on the center of her palm, feeding it from an eyedropper. Naked and bright pink, it was lapping vigorously, clutching the eyedropper between its front paws. Marly told me she had found it a few feet from the bodies of its mother and sibling, thrashing and crying in the roadside weeds.

As I peel the paper from my chopsticks, I say to Marly, "I've been thinking about your predilection for taking in strays."

Marly frowns in an irritated yet friendly way and refrains from responding.

"Like the two bunnies," I say. "Remember Uno and Dos? All the cats. And that baby possum."

"I was right to take in that possum, Mom. I still can't believe how cruel and callous you were." She says this with a smile. Three years later, she remains proud of her good deed. "But I know what you're trying to say, Mom: stray animals, maybe okay—stray men, not so good."

"Yes, exactly. Though I can see how the homeless man ended up out there."

We eat wonton soup, egg rolls, and chicken fried rice, and then return to Marly's apartment. The homeless man appears to be asleep. He looks as if he is sleeping lightly or else resting, maybe even faking. We tiptoe past him, and Marly turns the key in the lock to the lobby with a quiet click.

Still keeping quiet, we cross the lobby, and Marly lets us back into her apartment. She steps lightly across the living room to the kitchen, with me following, and makes us peppermint tea, and we sit down on the far-right side of the living room so as not to be exposed to the porch by the gap in the drapes. "I'm sick of hiding in my own apartment," Marly says, stroking Draven, a calico who was an outdoor cat at my house until last year, when Marly decided she was too old to live outside anymore.

"You can report him to the apartment manager," I suggest.

"Oh, Kirk is useless with things like that." She takes a sip of her tea. "I've been thinking of calling the police."

"You probably should, Marly. He can go live at the shelter. It's not really safe for you to have him living out there."

"I'm not worried about safe so much. All I have to do is give a shout, and my apartment mates will come running. But it's getting on my nerves. I feel like he's always watching me—or that he could be."

I stand and approach the curtain gap.

"Mom, don't!"

I hesitate, but then walk up to it and peek out. The couch is empty, the comforter scrunched like an abandoned cocoon. "He's gone."

"For now," Marly says. "Probably went to get some more booze." She drops her slender hand to her mug of tea and lifts it, closing her eyes to the warmth. We talk about her classes, and she strokes Draven, the old calico, who is settled on her lap. I stretch out my hand to Madison, the young pure-black cat, who appeared one morning mewling and with her ribs showing at Madison Manor; now she is sleek and happy and strolling across the back of the couch. "I wrote a poem a few days ago," Marly says. "Haven't written a poem since ninth grade. Want to see it?"

"Sure."

Marly lifts old Draven as if she is a delicate treasure and sets her aside on the couch, then stands and walks to her bedroom and returns with a sheet of notebook paper. "I was supposed to write a poem for my English class. But I'm not going to turn this one in."

She holds out the paper. It rattles in the quiet; even though Marly takes anti-anxiety meds, her hands still often shake. The title is handwritten at the top: **My Child's Soul**. I read the poem, remembering Marly two years ago: seventeen and pregnant by her boyfriend, who accompanied her to the clinic. I had gone, too, in a separate car, even though Marly hadn't wanted me there. What if she changed her mind and needed me for support? Or what if the procedure went awry? In either case, I wanted to be in the next room, not forty-five minutes distant. While Marly was under sedation, I sat in the waiting room, paging through magazines, alert. But all had gone according to plan, and afterward Marly was sure she had made the right decision.

The poem is both naked and matter-of-fact, in some places wordy, in others clean and sharp as a bone. But beyond all that, it's my child's poem. I re-read the last lines:

> *If a person's soul is the same size as the person*
> *My child's soul would fit on the palm of my hand.*

Marly's living room has grown dim. The sun is beginning to set, and the curtains block the light slanting in from the windows. "It's beautiful," I say.

"Don't get me wrong," Marly says. "I'm not sorry I had it done."

"You're not?"

"God, no. I wasn't ready for a kid. I'm still not ready for a kid. And it would have broken my heart to give her away to a pair of strangers. But I still feel a little sad about it sometimes."

"I feel the same way about mine," I tell her. I'd had the same procedure—an early abortion—when I was nineteen, the age Marly is now.

We sit in silence for a minute, Marly's small hands stroking Draven, who lies curled up and purring. Then Marly says, "Well, I should get to work on my paper. And I have to write another poem. One I won't mind showing to my teacher and the class."

I stand up from the couch. As I bend to pick up my empty tea mug, I see a flash of something in the curtain gap. Maybe it is just the setting sun. But I walk to the gap and, from inches away, peek out into the eyes of the homeless man. I let out a little cry and step back.

"What? Is he out there?"

"Yes, he is. Marly, he's looking in." I walk back over to Marly and lower my voice. "Did you know that the window is open? He was looking in through the screen."

Marly sits up straight. "That's it—I'm calling the police." She rummages in her purse for her phone. "That's happened before, but only in the daytime. He opened it to tell me that a delivery man had left a package." Instead of dialing, Marly sits holding the phone in her limp hand. "But maybe he didn't open it this time—Mitch might have left the window open."

"It doesn't matter who opened the window," I say. "He shouldn't be looking in."

"But if the police come out here, they might arrest him."

"Marly, you can't let this go on. Want me to call for you?"

"No."

"Well, what are you going to do?"

She draws in her breath and exhales. "I'll call them myself, I guess." She flips open the phone and dials.

"He hasn't hurt anyone, at all," she tells the operator. "All he's done is sleep on the couch on the porch and look in the window. Yeah, my boyfriend asked him to leave a couple of days ago."

Marly's kitchen is the size of a closet and lacks chairs, so we wait in the bedroom for the police to arrive. As we sit on Marly's bed, talking softly, we hear heavy footsteps thumping and creaking across the porch, voices, and then the homeless man shouting. "It's my friend who lives here! She lets me stay here! She's my friend!"

Marly looks at me in dismay. "Shit," she says. "He thinks I'm his friend. Crap! I probably am his only friend."

We wait, listening to the lowered voices of the policemen, whose words we can't hear, and to the homeless man shouting, "Ask my friend! She lives right there!"

"God, I feel terrible," Marly says.

There is a rap at the door. We both jump and then get up from the bed to answer it. A policeman with hooded eyes and chubby cheeks fills the doorway. "Are you the girl who called about the vagrant?" he asks.

"Yes," Marly says, "but he hasn't done anything really wrong. Maybe I should have asked him to leave myself— maybe he would have listened to me."

"Well, don't feel too bad about it," the policeman says. "You're not the first young lady whose window he's been looking in. We've had several other complaints from this neighborhood."

"About that same guy?" Marly asks.

"Well, we don't know for sure. But he fits the description."

After the police leave, I ask Marly if she wants to spend the night at my house. "No. I'm fine. I mostly feel bad for the guy. I hope they don't keep him long. And I hope they don't tell him that I'm the one who called the police."

"They won't tell him," I reassure her. "They don't give out information that might lead someone to retaliate."

"I'm not worried about retaliation," Marly says. "I just don't want him thinking that it was his friend who turned him in." She gathers up our empty mugs. "Why do things have to get so complicated?" she asks.

I resist repeating what my mother would say. But I can't think of what to say instead, so I quote my mom after all: "Your Grandma would say, 'That's life.'"

"Yeah, well sometimes life sucks."

"It does," I agree. "But luckily it doesn't all the time."

"Yeah, well I think it sucks way too often."

"Less would be better," I say, trying to agree without being too negative.

Marly's lips are set in a thin line, and her eyes are dark and clouded. She carries the mugs out to the kitchen and sets them down. We talk about our schedules for the coming week. Then she walks me to the lobby, where she gives me her usual brief yet tight hug, her bony fingers pressing into my back. I kiss her on the side of her head, behind her right eye, wishing I had more to say.

On the drive home, I think of the possum that Marly held on her hand, on her open palm, as small as the soul of the child in her poem. Too young to exist outside its mother's pouch, the possum had died after a day and a half. And I remember the adult fox Marly found one day in the road, walking in circles, stumbling as if drunk. She wrapped it in her jacket, placed it on the floor of her car, drove home, and called the vet. The vet didn't want to treat the animal; he told Marly to call the Department of Natural Resources. The DNR employee who answered the phone said it sounded as if the fox had distemper and that Marly could drive it to their facility in Kalamazoo and they would euthanize it there, or she could put it down herself. Marly decided that rather than drive for over an hour with the sick fox in her car, she would put it to death.

"It was so hard, Mom," she told me later. She had taken the fox into the furnace room—she was living at home then, and I was at work—and had pressed a pillow over its face. "I figured he was so weak, I could smother him easily," she told me. "But even though he could hardly stand up, he had a lot of life left in him. He struggled for a long time."

Marly was sixteen then. She was thirteen when she and the neighborhood kids rescued the bunnies they named Uno and Dos. As I drive toward home on the expressway from Marly's apartment, gliding past dark slopes and fields lying under the starred sky, I remember that rescue attempt. It was an attempt that worked, at least in part: one stray was saved, and then later released. Uno is buried under a bush or pine that the kids have forgotten. Dos is also dead—even if he managed to elude the neighborhood dogs and lived a long life and fathered many baby rabbits, he would be long dead by now of old age. But at least for a while, he thrived. He grew into a fast, supple, angular adolescent, and when the teenagers who raised him decided it was time to let him go, they whooped and laughed and cheered as he bounded off into the wild grass.

Loveland Pass

I'M SITTING AROUND with two of my women friends one evening when Karen says, "Nina, tell Annie about that guy who was housesitting for you! He sounds like he would be perfect for Annie!"

"Well, I don't usually play matchmaker, but ..." Nina takes a sip of her wine. She teaches psychology at Hope College, a small Christian school twelve miles north of our town. "I have this colleague—Richard Kanelos—maybe you know him?"

I shake my head.

"He housesat for Camden and me last week while we were in Georgia. He's been teaching English at Hope for, oh, about twenty years, and he's recently divorced."

"Annie, did you hear that?" Karen says. "He teaches English! Hey, I wonder if he's a writer!"

"I don't know if he is or not," Nina says. "I don't think so."

"If he's been at Hope for twenty years," I say, "I wonder why I've never met him." I set down my glass, and Karen pours in more wine. I took a few classes at Hope long ago, and through the years I've attended dozens of Hope readings, and I've also read there twice myself.

Nina says that Richard doesn't go to many social functions, and that's probably why I've never run across him. "He has four kids," she explains, "and, until recently, a wife, and they took up most of his time."

"Well, what does he look like?" Karen asks. "Is he good-looking?"

Nina knits her brow. "He has a nice face. Black hair that's turning gray. A beard, I think."

"What about his body?" Karen asks. "Is he fit?"

Nina's brow furrows further. "He doesn't look like a couch potato, exactly. He's kind of average, I guess. Short and squat."

"Short and squat!" Karen crows. She's on her third glass of wine. The two of us burst out laughing, and Nina soon joins us.

"Don't quit your job and go into matchmaking!" I tease. Then I mimic Nina's professorial voice: "I've found the perfect man for you. He's average. Not a couch potato, exactly."

"And short and squat!" Karen shouts.

After we've quieted down, Nina says, "I think you would find how Richard looks appealing enough. And while I don't know him all that well, I think if I did, he would be my friend." Nina tells me a little more about Richard, and then she offers to invite Richard and me, along with Karen and her boyfriend, over for dinner with Nina and her husband. But sitting down with two committed couples sounds like too much pressure to me, so I come up with a plan of my own. That night I call Jerry, a friend and former teacher of mine who teaches poetry at Hope, and propose that I stop by to borrow a book the following week, when Richard will be house-sitting for him.

"Then we can just chat," I say, "and there won't be any pressure on either of us. If I don't like him, he never needs to know that I came over for anything but the book."

Jerry laughs. "That's a slick plan! What book do you want to borrow?"

"I'm not sure—what do you have?"

"Well, are you looking for poetry—or prose?"

"Let's go with prose," I say.

"Have you read *The Natural History of Love*, by Diane Ackerman?"

"I think it would be better to leave 'love' out of the title. Remember, this is just a straightforward errand."

"Oh, I hadn't thought of that!" Jerry laughs again and suggests some short fiction by Joy Williams. I tell him, sure, I like her stories, and I've only read a couple.

"Okay, then," Jerry says, "we've got a strategy!"

Before hanging up, we decide that, rather than borrowing just one of Williams's books, I will borrow them both, since stopping by for two books will make my errand seem weightier.

Several days later, on a warm August evening, Richard answers Jerry's front door and invites me in. He is heavier than most of the men I have dated—Nina was right when she described him as squat—but his weight is spread evenly over his body, and his bearded face is broad rather than fat, and his smile is easy and open.

"So, you've come for some books," he says. "Jerry said to expect you. He didn't say where they were, though. Let's go check the shelves."

I follow Richard into the study, a large room with a desk and chair at one end, a couch at the center, and bookshelves covering the better part of three walls. "They don't seem to be arranged in any particular order," Richard says. We are standing near the largest shelf, and, as we run our fingers over the titles, we begin to chat. Forty minutes later, after more chatting than looking, we find the books, having passed over them at least once. I pull the soft paperbacks from the shelf, but neither of us says anything about me leaving, now that my errand is completed. Instead, Richard and I walk over to the long, deep couch and settle down at its opposite ends, and the conversation shifts from books and people we know in common to Richard's recent divorce.

It is still fresh—it became final nine months ago, just before Christmas—and his divorce and its aftermath is the subject most on his mind. Richard tells me that his wife informed him during the winter before last that she wanted him to move out. She said she knew on their wedding day, nearly twenty years ago, that the marriage was a mistake—because, she said, Richard wasn't a serious, ambitious person—but so as not to disrupt the children's school year, they continued to live together last year as usual until summer vacation arrived.

Richard rubs the underside of his beard. "The twins were about to move out anyway, into dorm rooms at their college. I offered to stay in the house with the boys, since, besides having more money, I'm a steadier person than their mother. But she said if I tried to get custody, she would fight me to the death—those were her actual words—and I didn't want to put the boys through that."

"That's a tough situation," I say, keeping my other thought to myself: if it were me, I would have fought.

"And how was *your* divorce?" Richard asks.

I pause, considering his choice of words and inflection, and I guess he considers them, too: we both laugh.

"Actually," I say, "it was easy, as divorces go. Ray and I both wanted to share custody of our daughter equally, and we didn't argue about anything else. We were so on the same page that we even used the same lawyer. But Marly burst into the most desolate tears when we told her. And while it was good that she got to live with both of us, I think boucing back and forth between our two houses was somewhat unsettling for her."

Richard says he knows how it feels to not have a single place to call home, and he explains his own unusual living situation, which he "lucked into" last fall: for ten months of the year, he gets to live rent-free in a guest cottage on a dune overlooking Lake Michigan in exchange for watching over the main house while the owners winter in Florida; the unlucky part is that during July and August he has to find somewhere else to live, and during this summer he has had to pick up and move, every week or two, to a different place.

We've been conversing for a couple of hours when Richard says he would love to keep talking, but he still has to prepare for the summer class he is teaching the next morning. We get up from the couch, and Richard walks me to the door. He holds out his hand, and I shake it, surprised and a bit dismayed that he doesn't offer me a hug. But his voice is warm as he says good-bye, and he looks right into my face. He doesn't seem squat to me anymore, but nicely broad and not too tall, and, as Nina suggested, handsome enough. And I like his narrow, dark eyes, which seem at once sexy and kind. We don't exchange phone numbers or arrange to meet again. But I feel fairly certain that something has started between us.

⌒

FOR OUR FIRST DATE, we get together for coffee in Saugatuck.
Next we go out to a movie, and then Richard invites himself
over for dinner. One Sunday after we've been dating for about a
month, we drive an hour north of Grand Rapids to the Wheat-
land Music Festival. When was the last time, I wonder, that a
man wanted to spend a whole Sunday with me? I think of a
song I like by Etta James: "I want a Sunday kind of Love." That's
what I want; Sunday and Monday as well as any other day or
night of the week that we wish to spend together.

Not long after, we spend the night in the guest cottage
Richard has moved back into, and we make love for the first
time. I've changed my mind about waiting to have sex until
I'm sure a relationship will last. There is no way of being sure,
and it's begun to seem unnatural to hold off from being fully
sexual for months, or a year, or however long I think I might
need to be more sure but still not certain. It's enough that we
seem like a good match and that Richard talks as if our being
together in the forseeable future is a given.

We begin spending our nights in the lakeside room that
the owners of the cottage have dubbed "the best bedroom in
West Michigan," because it has two walls of windows so close
to the lake that nothing is visible but water and sky. Being in
the room reminds me of when I first moved to southwest
Michigan and stayed in a cabin overlooking the lake with Ray,
and also later, during our marriage, when we lived up the road
in the camp manager's house, from which we could still hear
the lake when the waves were high.

Above the headboard of Richard's bed is a print of a great
horned owl settled onto the branch of a white pine—it's the

same print that hung over the bed I shared with Ray. Ray and I bought the print when we were newly married, and we sold it during our divorce; Richard's copy of the print was placed there by the owners of the cottage. When I tell Richard that that same owl picture hung over my marriage bed, he offers to remove it. "No, I really like that picture," I say. "It's kind of nice to have it back." The walls surrounding the print, knotty pine, are also like those in the room I shared with my husband, over a decade ago and just a few miles down the beach, and lying next to Richard with the waves rolling in, I feel that I've returned in some way to my earlier life, and that I'm being given another chance: to live by the lake again, and to get love right. One night lying nestled in bed with Richard, I tell him, "This is the best bedroom in West Michigan, but not just because of the view."

"Oh, that's sweet," Richard says, wrapping me closer. "I agree."

RICHARD AND I have been a couple for three months when we drive up to Holland to hear Matthew, Richard's thirteen-year-old son, play in his school concert. Richard sends me in ahead to claim seats for us while he parks his van. When I walk into the auditorium, I see Richard's other three children, his college-age twin girls and ten-year-old Luke, all of whom I've met, sitting with a woman I don't recognize but know must be their mother. Cassie and Jess smile and nod at me from across the room, and Luke's eyes light up and he waves. I wave back, grateful and relieved to be acknowledged and even welcomed by Richard's children. Their mother does not wave or act as if she sees me, but we haven't met or even glimpsed each other before this, and we are separated now by a dozen rows of seats. I take in Beth briefly, noting her stylish clothes and her rounded, voluptuous body. Richard has told me that Beth has put on so many pounds in recent years that he finds her grotesque, so I'm surprised to discover that, while she is broader than Richard, who is himself a bit chubby, she is only moderately heavy, and that, far from grotesque, she looks attractive and sexy.

After the concert, as we are filing out of the auditorium, Richard halts and says, "Oh, I forgot I need to tell Matthew something. I'll meet you in the hallway." But as soon as I have drifted with the other concert-goers out into the hall, I spot Matthew, who is tall for thirteen and looming above the crowd, standing by a far wall with Luke and their mother. Although Beth and I haven't been introduced, I know that Richard regularly chats with Beth's boyfriend, so I walk up and say, "Matthew, your dad is looking for you—he thinks you're still in the auditorium." Then, as Matthew strides off, I face Beth and say, "Hi, I'm Annie."

Beth looks away from me—she turns her head to the side and squints off into space and doesn't speak. Even before the squint, I've noticed that her eyes are narrow, like Richard's. I stand watching her for a few seconds, then glance at Luke. His own narrow blue eyes are looking uncomfortably off in the other direction, even though when I ran into him at the drinking fountain during the concert, he joked with me and held up his hand for a high five. I glance back at Beth, who is still squinting off to the side as if I'm a homeless person who has strayed into her yard. Well, I *am* wearing an old pair of jeans and a slightly worn black jacket I picked up at Goodwill, but my hair is freshly washed and I think I must look fairly normal. Beth is wearing a new, sleek black coat that stops above her shapely calves. Her dyed blond hair is short and styled, and her face is heavily made up—a deep red lipstick exaggerates the curves of her lips, and a layer of blush and foundation coats her face. As always, I'm wearing no makeup, and my naturally wavy brown hair is slightly messy and threaded with gray. Now I understand why Richard exclaimed, on one of our first dates: "That's what I like about you—there's absolutely no hype!" He hadn't been describing me so much as comparing me to his ex-wife. As we stand face-to-face with Beth's face averted, I try again to break the ice: "I thought Matthew played really well. I especially liked that second number." Beth continues to squint, waiting for me to disappear. Her mouth remains motionless, set in a thin, hard line. I notice with a mean flash of pleasure that even though she's dyed her hair a youthful blond and we're right around the same age, she looks ten years older than me. "Well, I guess I'll talk to you later," I say, and, stepping back, I find a place to stand near the opposite wall.

Driving home in the van I complain to Richard: "You'd think, for the kids' sake if nothing else, she would try to act more cordial."

Richard says that Beth doesn't intend to be rude, that she is just terrible in public and in new situations.

"She's the one who asked for the divorce," I counter. "And she began dating right away. What does she think, that you sit home grading papers by yourself every night? I mean, she knows you're dating me, right?"

"Yes."

"Well, I'm sure that meeting your ex-husband's girlfriend might make a person feel awkward. But it's weird that she didn't just mumble hi to me. I think it took more effort *not* to speak to me."

"She just doesn't know how to act," Richard says. "She never has. I wouldn't take it personally."

Richard has already told me that Beth suffers from depression and other health issues that are vague and hard to pinpoint, some of them real, and others hypochondriacal. She spent whole months of the kids' childhoods lying on the couch or simply staying in bed. Richard taught a full load of college courses, then came home and made dinner, took care of the kids, and cleaned the house. Sometimes he left work early in order to care for the kids, and he took more days off than he was entitled to. But rather than being thankful for any of his extra efforts, Beth complained that he didn't make enough money and was not ambitious.

"It seems like you should have been the one asking for the divorce," I say as Richard steers his van up the winding road to the cottage.

Richard coasts up to the cottage and turns off the engine. "I didn't want to do that to the kids," he says. "And I'm kind of old-fashioned. I took my marriage vows seriously."

Although the van's windows are closed, we can hear the lake roaring. "You mean, in sickness and in health?"

Richard nods, staring out at the black lake. "Till death do us part."

⌣

ONE SUNDAY MY DAUGHTER drives down from Grand Rapids and eats dinner with us. Richard asks Marly about college, and she tells him about her classes, especially her favorite, black and white photography. As she tells Richard about her latest photos and as Richard heartily responds, I wait for Marly to glance at me and telegraph her amusement or disdain. But she is too engrossed in their conversation to send me any signals.

After Richard leaves, I ask Marly what she thinks of him. "I like him a lot," she says. "He's really nice." Until now, during the fourteen years since her father and I split up, Marly's comments on my boyfriends have ranged from "he's a dork," to "he's okay, I guess," to "seems like a nutcase, Mom."

"Well, I'm glad you like Richard," I say, "because I haven't been so serious about anyone in . . . in all the years I've been divorced." In truth, it seems I've never been so serious about anyone, ever, but for Marly's sake, I don't want to place Richard above her dad.

"I think he'd be a good one for you to marry," Marly says. She pushes back a wing of her stop-sign-red hair. "Though I have to admit that his whole whacked-out Christian thing kind of scares me."

"He's not a strict Christian anymore," I say.

"It worries me that he ever was one. And also, I think it's really weird that, growing up when he did—I mean, c'mon, Mom, he was a teenager in the late sixties—he *never once* smoked weed."

"He says that no one ever offered it to him."

"Yeah, well, what does that say about him?" Marly asks. "Still, out of all the weirdos and whackos you've brought home, he's the best by far."

⌒

RICHARD IS NEVER HAPPIER than when he has all four of his children with him at once, and he is especially thrilled to have them at his house the first Christmas Eve after we meet. I am happy, too, at being included in the celebration, and at being in a relationship that is going so very well.

"Who's ready for Chef Richard's incredible moussaka?" Richard asks, holding the battered aluminum pan he's found among the cottage's meager kitchen accoutrements in one hand and a big, splayed metal flipper in the other. Jess, who is sitting closest to the pan, holds up her plate.

Richard serves everyone squares of moussaka, and we pass salad and garlic bread, which is burned around the edges, and begin to eat. "Nice burn job on the bread, Dad," Matthew says.

"I was trying for a flambé-type effect," Richard answers.

"The difference between a little burned and perfect is, like, one second," Cassie says, defending her father. "You literally have to sit in front of the broiler and keep your eye on it without blinking."

Jess, who wants to be an artist and rarely speaks unless spoken to, breaks the burned edges from her bread and deposits them on Matthew's plate.

"Hey, thanks a lot, Jess," Matthew says.

Jess grins in reply.

"Whose music are we listening to?" Richard asks.

"Mine," Jess says.

"Do you mind taking it off and putting on that new CD I bought for Annie? She hasn't heard it yet."

"Did you pick it out, or did Annie?" Matthew asks as Jess rises from her seat.

"I did," Richard says. "I gave it to her for Christmas."

"It's not Christmas music, is it?" Matthew asks.

"No," Richard says.

"Or *Christian* music?"

"I've never bought any Christian music."

"No, you just purged the Satanic stuff, right Dad? Can you believe he got rid of Earth, Wind and Fire?" Matthew says to me without waiting for his dad to answer. Matthew has needled his dad about this before in my presence, and Richard has admitted that he had, at Beth's request, culled certain records from his collection. "Thank God," Mathew says, "no, I mean, *thank Satan* that he's gotten over his Christian phase." As I half-successfully stifle a laugh, the first few notes of a song I've heard many times but have forgotten float in over the open counter dividing the living room from the kitchen.

"I know this song," I say, looking over at Richard, who has left his seat beside me to bring the wine to the table. "And I really like it. But I can't remember what it is."

I listen to a few more notes. "It's one that Etta James sings," I say, "but it's not her version of it."

A lovely voice unfamiliar to me joins the piano:

At Last,
My love has come along;
My lonely days are over,
And life is like a song.

I sit very still, taking in the whole room with my peripheral vision, the twins and the boys, the old, hodge-podge cottage furniture and knotty pine walls, the overhead lights and the lamps in the corners, the darkness outside the kitchen windows, and Richard sitting so close to me now that I can feel him more than see him. For a moment, all I hear is the song. Then Luke is telling Matthew about a skateboard video game, and Cassie is asking Jess to pass the salad.

"I love this song," I say, leaning closer to Richard, my cheek brushing the edge of his beard.

"It can be ours, if you want," Richard says next to my ear.

I turn my head so that I can see him. He is smiling, his narrow eyes shining. "Yes," he says, "let's call it ours."

⌣

ONE EVENING WHEN I meet Richard at his house, he tells me that he thinks he's found the thing he is meant to do. "It's poetry," he says bashfully, looking up from his recliner, books and papers scattered all around him. "Not just reading it, but writing it. I might not ever be very good at it. But I took out some of the poems I wrote right after my divorce, and I've started working on them, and it gives me the greatest feeling."

He begins getting up early every morning to write, and in the middle of March, I board a plane for Colorado with Richard's first batch of finished poems in my carry-on bag. I am flying out to meet him at the end of a conference he is attending in Denver, and from there we will drive up into the mountains to spend four days with his older sister. Richard has told me that he wants me to read his poems for the first time while I am up in the sky, so I wait until the plane has leveled off above the field of clouds that stretches in all directions, hiding the ground below.

His poems speak vaguely of being wounded and beginning to heal since his divorce, but they are concrete only in their descriptions of trillium and geese and Lake Michigan. I like parts of all of them and a few in their entirety, but I'm not so interested in hearing about nature as about Richard's life; I want a key to what lies deep inside him. But he hasn't travelled that far inward yet, or, if he has, he is sharing only glimpses.

I also hope to find out what he thinks of and feels for me—I'm hoping for at least one love poem among the packet. But while there is no such poem, there is a note. In it he writes: **These poems more or less form a progression, as arranged, from melancholic, to less so, to the new roots of my first, long-awaited joys, in large part because of you in my life. This is very fun, and so are you, and so is my loving of you very much.**

I reread the note, then look out the jet's window at the vast plain of clouds below. I've been wanting, ever since my marriage ended, to meet a man who would love me this whole-heartedly. I write in my journal, look out at the clouds, read the note again.

When the plane touches down, several hours late, Richard is waiting for me at the baggage claim. I run into his arms and hug him fiercely, and then we collect my luggage and rent a car and drive through the ink-black night up into the mountains. "It's too bad you're seeing this in the dark," Richard says. "Missing the views. But you'll get to see it in daylight when we come back down."

Richard has trouble sleeping that night, because of the altitude—we are eleven thousand feet above sea level, several thousand feet above the comfort level for many lowland dwellers. I discover him sitting on the living room couch, trying to read, at six in the morning. He has been there since around four—he finds he can breathe more easily sitting up. His face is whitish-gray, as if he has the flu.

Richard's brother-in-law is prepared for visitors who succumb to altitude sickness, and on the second night of our visit, he sets up an oxygen tank beside our bed, and Richard threads the plastic tubes into his nostrils. He falls asleep quickly, but when I wake up to use the bathroom early in the morning, he is back on the couch, sitting up, looking gray and reading to keep his mind off his breathing. The tank, which he thought would last for eight hours, ran out after four. He didn't know how to hook up the second tank, and he didn't want to wake his brother-in-law to ask him.

During the following days, we ride a gondola up into the mountains and hike around a bit and drive to see the sights. And I take long walks through the pines and snow, by myself and with Richard's sister, while Richard, still gray-faced but uncomplaining, sits on the couch with a magazine in front of his face.

After four days, we say good-bye, get back into our rental car, and head east and down. I offer to drive, but Richard says that I'm not used to mountain driving and he is fine. The car descends and climbs and curves around the mountains. At Loveland Pass, we stop and get out. Richard is so subdued that I don't make a comment about standing with him at Loveland Pass and so gray that I don't try to kiss him. The farther mountains are hemmed in by clouds, but the closer ones are clearly visible. No wonder they are called the Rocky Mountains—there is nothing to them but rock, no visible earth or grass or trees. They look old and harsh yet beautiful. Still, I prefer the lower mountains, which are living and green.

From Loveland Pass we descend farther, each switchback and loop winding us downward. In Georgetown, we stop for lunch in a Victorian house that has been converted into a restaurant. We order the day's special, bowls of Irish lamb stew, and, as we are eating, the color comes back into Richard's face.

I've gotten so used to his grayness that the pink of his cheeks surprises me. Along with the color in his cheeks, forehead, and neck, life has come back into his eyes—I hadn't noticed how dull and flat they'd grown until I see their liveliness return. As he voraciously eats the stew, he drinks me in with his gleaming gaze.

When we reach Denver, we check into the motel where we'll spend the night before our return flight. It is early afternoon and the day is sunny and mild, so I suggest a walk, but Richard grins and shakes his head, then pulls me to the bed, and we strip off our clothes and make love with extra gusto.

"Nice to have you back, sweetie," I say afterward, my arms still circling his neck. "I hadn't realized what a zombie you'd become. Or is it that motel rooms turn you on?"

"Breathing turns me on," Richard says. "And you, of course. Sorry I've been such a wet blanket this whole trip."

"You've been great this whole trip," I say. "If I were you, I would have been miserable, and not so good at hiding it."

"I still had fun," Richard says, "but, man, it's great to breathe and to make love to you again."

⌣

MY LITTLE SISTER is getting married that May, in Detroit. "Will you dance with me at Nicole's wedding?" I ask Richard when we are making our plans. He hesitates and then says yes.

I know Richard doesn't like dancing in public, so I figure he'll dance a token dance or maybe two, but he dances with me for the whole two hours the band plays, smiling into my eyes.

I smile back at him, looking in deep. We'll have dancing at our wedding, when the time comes—we've been talking about our wedding as if it is a given, although we haven't made any plans or set any timetable for it. But I don't really care about the wedding itself. I wish that I was already married to him. I wish I had met him when we were in our twenties and that we married then and had our children together. But marrying him in the near future will be nearly as good: I will get to live out the second half of my life with him.

When it comes time for my sister to throw her bouquet, one of my sisters-in-law gives me a little push, and I join the other single women on the cleared dance floor. I am forty-three, the oldest among them. I stand with my hands at my sides rather than raised, as the younger women and girls are doing. Some are lifting up onto their toes, and one girl is jumping in place. I stand flat on my feet. I'll only try to catch it if it comes directly my way. I feel funny even being out on the floor and trying at my age, and I don't want to seem too eager. Yet I hope the flowers will sail to me and float right into my hands.

My sister flings the bouquet over her shoulder, and it hurtles, ribbons streaming, straight toward my niece Ruth, who is seventeen and very beautiful. She catches it and whoops.

⌒

IN JUNE, AS WE HAVE for the past seven summers, my family holds our reunion at the camp where I lived and worked when I first moved to Saugatuck. Richard has to teach a summer seminar every morning that week, but he joins us each evening for dinner and stays for our campfires, and after the first day, Matthew and Luke go home and get their sleeping bags and a few changes of clothing and move into a cabin with me.

With Richard absent except in the evenings, I become the boys' surrogate parent. They give me the rocks they collect from the beach, tell me when they are going into town with my nieces and nephews, and come looking for me when they have nothing else to do. I teach Mathew how to sail a Sunfish, and I build sandcastles with Luke. I wake them for breakfast, round them up at lunchtime, and at dinnertime I save them seats, along with one for their dad. At night, bedded down on separate cots but in the same small room, I listen to Luke breathing peacefully and to Matthew muttering in his sleep.

After the reunion, Matthew and Luke go on a week-long vacation with their mother, and when they return, they won't meet my gaze. I have dinner with Richard and the boys as usual the Wednesday evening after they get back, and whenever I speak to either Matthew or Luke, they answer briefly, not meeting my eyes, looking down at their plates or with their heads angled away from me. After Richard has returned from taking the boys back home to their mother, I meet him in the kitchen. "I don't know if Beth said something to the boys," I say, "or if she got it across by her behavior, but it's obvious—she's made it clear—that she won't accept their being friendly to me."

"I don't think she would do that," Richard says.

"Didn't you notice how they avoided talking to me during dinner?" I ask.

"Maybe they were tired, or had other things on their minds."

"No, they were clearly uncomfortable. They wouldn't even look at me."

"I don't think Beth would say anything," Richard says.

"She wouldn't have to *say* anything," I say. "They probably came back from the camp talking about all the fun things they did with my family and me, and she shut them down, she turned away from them, the same way that they are now turning away from me."

Not long after this, we run into Beth at Luke's indoor soccer practice. It is Richard's weekend with the boys, but Beth has shown up anyway, as she often does. Her usual habit, Richard later tells me, is to sit next to Richard and discuss their children, but because I'm there, she sits alone, except for when I walk off to use the bathroom.

As I'm returning, I notice that Beth has left her seat and is now sitting on the bleacher right where I had left my coat. Alarm and anger flare in me—she has pushed my coat aside, she is sitting in my place! I tell myself to calm down, that nothing is amiss. But Matthew is hunched sullenly between his parents, gazing at his feet, while Beth speaks rapidly, her red lips stretching in her angry face, and Richard is wearing a pasted-on look of dutiful concern that doesn't hide his dread. Warily, my heart beating fast, I step down the stairs, past six rows of empty seats, until I am only three aisles above them, to one side but in earshot.

"You should never have brought him here," Beth says. "You were just thinking of yourself, as usual, forgetting what's best for him." Later Richard tells me that Beth was berating him for bringing Matthew, who hates sports, to Luke's practice. Richard tried to explain to her that Matthew tagged along, as I did also, because we were going straight from Luke's soccer practice to an international dinner at the college. But Beth hadn't been appeased.

"Did you even ask if they wanted to go?" she says as I stand above them, still off to the side and unnoticed. "You know they hate those rubbery mushrooms and slimy sauces! And, let me guess, you're bringing those greasy little honey pastries that stick in your throat."

I want to rush up and defend Richard; I want to call Beth

an unappreciative bitch and tell her to take her fat, interfering ass back to her own seat. I also consider turning around and returning to the bathroom and waiting till this is finished. I haven't seen Beth since that one time at Matthew's concert, when I introduced myself and she stayed silent. But rather than retreating or approaching, I stay where I am, looking down and over at Beth, who has her back to me, her big butt nudging my coat as she continues her harangue. I think of what my father, a plain-speaking psychiatrist, said to me about Richard and Beth: "He's afraid of her. She's got him by the balls."

I make my way closer, stepping past the last empty bleachers that separate them from me. When I am in the same aisle and only ten feet away from her, Beth rises to her feet. Then she straightens her broad body and swivels in my direction. I hang back, looking off to the side, trying to act as if I haven't noticed her harassing her ex-husband. Beth looks past me rather than at me, her lips stretched in distaste, and I can't pretend any longer, my mouth turns as bitter as hers. Then something unexpected happens: for the first time, our eyes meet. Hers are infused with a cold fury. They stop on mine for only a second, and then she is looking past me again. We are facing each other, but not looking at each other—I am just like her now, unable to look her in the eye or even glance at her face. If either of us turned sideways and shrank, the other could pass, but she has puffed herself up like a blowfish and is waiting for me to retreat up the aisle, and I have squared myself off, also unwilling to back down. I haven't been in a fight since I was a teenager, and then it was in self-defense. Well, maybe this is self-defense, too—and defense of Richard and Matthew. My fingernails would have to dig to reach to the skin beneath the makeup on Beth's face; I would have to hit her squarely so my fist wouldn't slide off the surface. She weighs more than me, but we are the same height, and her extra weight is only blubber. I'm not sure which of the two of us is fiercer.

But this isn't truly self-defense, and I don't really want to fight her—it would only make matters worse. Besides, she is Richard's past, and I am his present and his future. I turn sideways and shrink to let her pass.

"I'll call you, Rich," she says, leaning close to his face. He nods, hanging his head. "Bye, Mattie." She pats Matthew's head, which is also hanging, eyes clouded with tears. Then she brushes by me, her strong, sickly-sweet perfume invading my nostrils, her gaze pointedly blank; it's as if she thinks that by not registering my presence, she can make me disappear. Or maybe it is something more elemental than that, which I feel now as well: anger at—and fear of—the other's very existence. Maybe that's what lies at the heart of our aversion: her inability—and now mine—to face or accept a rival.

⌒

Two MONTHS LATER, in August, after Richard and I have been together for almost a year, I drive north, through the increasingly hilly landscape, to a cottage on Lake Michigan that belongs to Richard's older brother. Like the caretaker's house, this cottage is also very close to the water, perched on a dune just above the beach and the waves. There are no nearby trees, only dune grass and sand, and such openess makes the sky and the lake seem even vaster and closer. Richard is spending the week at his brother's cottage alone, except for the three days that I join him. He comes out of the house grinning when I pull into the driveway, and as soon as we go inside, he uncorks a bottle of wine. "To our vacation," he says. "To three whole days of relaxing and recreating." We clink glasses, and he draws me close and kisses me. His enthusiasm remains high throughout our dinner preparations. I'm excited, too, for another reason besides our getting to spend a few days vacationing together, and I think Richard will be pleased, too, when I tell him why.

I wait until we are relaxing on the porch overlooking the lake with plates of his grilled chicken and my ziti with pesto. Then I say, "There's something I've been looking forward to telling you. I've been thinking a lot about Beth's behavior, about her attitude toward me—toward us—and I've stopped feeling angry at her. I realize now that she behaves the way she does not out of meanness, but from fear. Like the way she won't look at me, or acknowledge that I exist. Or how she won't let us keep the boys for even an extra hour. I know that part of her behavior is calculating. But it's fear that's behind it."

Richard looks as deflated as if someone has just told him that his winning lottery ticket is no good after all—he likes to go to sleep at night imagining what he'd do if he won a million dollars.

"This is a good, thing, sweetie," I say. "Now that I've stopped being angry, I can live with the way things are, for now. Which means that we don't necessarily have to wait till the boys are grown to get married." We've both thought that it might be better to wait till Beth is more removed from Richard's life to get married.

Richard is looking across the table at me uneasily, his hand holding his wine glass as if he's forgotten it. He had brought up marriage first, and he's mentioned it more often than I have, and when I raised the option of just living together, he said that he was "too old to play house." But Richard hasn't brought up marriage lately. In fact, I can't remember when he mentioned it last.

I continue to try to explain to Richard how my new understanding and attitude will keep Beth from being an impediment to our relationhip. Finally Richard answers: "It might not be so easy."

"Well, I know Beth isn't going to change," I say. "But my attitude toward her has changed, and I think that will make a huge difference. Not in her life, but in ours."

"I don't know the answer to that," Richard says. "But I don't want to talk about it right now."

During our following days together, Richard seems troubled. I don't take much note of it, I'm so pleased with the easing of my anger toward Beth, and about Richard and me being on vacation, just the two of us, right on the lake. The water and air are a little chilly for swimming, so we spend most of our days at the cottage reading and writing, sitting side by side on the deck facing the lake when the weather permits, and sitting across from each other on the living room's twin couches when it is rainy or cool. On our third afternoon together, facing Richard from the opposite couch as rain drizzles the deck and pricks the lake's surface, I look up from my journal. "I love sitting here with you," I say. "Looking up and seeing you across the room. I love just looking at you."

Richard glances up from the book on his lap. "Sometimes you look at me too much," he says quietly.

I look back down at my notebook, dismissing what he has just said, still so enveloped by my happy bubble that his words don't really penetrate. Probably I've spoken too sentimentally, I think.

◡

ON THE LAST SATURDAY in October, Richard holds a sunset party at his new house, a lakeside cabin he is renting for the winter season. The party starts at five, but I have to work till six-thirty, so I'm the last guest to arrive. Before the potluck, Richard and I discussed what he was making and what I would bring, and, knowing I would be late, I asked him to save me a piece of his grilled chicken.

When I step into the kitchen, it is almost empty—most of the guests are in the living room and outside. Richard walks past me without stopping to greet me, his face distracted yet nearly blank, and says in an offhand voice, "Oh, I forgot to save you chicken."

In the awkward pause that follows, I take in the room around me. Sitting in the middle of the kitchen floor is a friend and colleague of Richard's whom I met at an English department party soon after I met Richard. Rebecca has shoulder-length blond hair and a narrow face with sharp features, and now, as before, she wears a long dress that nips in at her tiny waist. Her face is too angular to be pretty, but she looks fresh and youthful—she is in her early thirties, ten years younger than me—and although she seems to me painfully thin, I've noticed that men who are slightly heavy like Richard tend to find extreme thinness attractive. Because they are colleagues, Richard and Rebecca have the same work schedules, including weekends off, and it looks as if Rebecca has been at this party for most or all of it so far. She is sitting on the floor with her youngest daughter, who is wearing a dress to match her mother's, unhurriedly helping her little girl straighten her socks and retie her shoes.

At the party at which I met her, Rebecca asked me in a careful tone that seemed meant to sound casual, "Who all do you know here?" I listed half the members of the English department and then said, "And Richard, of course." Rebecca's sharp face had fallen. Later that evening, when Richard excused himself to use the bathroom, he turned to me and said he'd be right back, and then he turned to Rebecca, who was sitting on a stool at his other side, and, as if to say the same thing but wordlessly, he rubbed her thigh through her dress. Afterward, Richard told me that the party seemed like our coming-out party as a couple, and that all of his colleagues who knew us were so happy for us, so I didn't say anything about his hand on Rebecca's leg. I reasoned that his touch was a sort of apology to Rebecca, for passing over her and choosing me instead.

Rebecca's name has come up again since then—Richard told me they used to meet for lunch "to trade war stories" while they were both going through their divorces, and during the last school year and a couple of times so far this year as well, he has stopped by her house after work for Thank-God-It's-Friday parties. When Richard and I first started dating, Rebecca's divorce wasn't final. But it became final a few months ago, and after one of Rebecca's recent parties, which Richard attended while I was still at work, I confided to Richard that I was afraid he might leave me for Rebecca.

"She's not my type," Richard answered. We were in his van, approaching Rebecca's huge Victorian mansion, which is situated only one street over from where Matthew and Luke live with their mother and just a few blocks from Hope College. Richard had recently exclaimed to me that Rebecca's house has ten bedrooms; in contrast, my house has only one spare bedroom, Marly's big old attic room, which Richard has deemed too small for his boys to share. Richard has also recently lamented that my house is "way out in the boondocks," far from Hope College and the boys' schools.

"Well, she must be at least somewhat your type," I said as the car rolled by Rebecca's enormous yellow and orange mansion, "or you wouldn't have rubbed her leg." Rather than turn his head toward Rebecca's bright behemoth, Richard kept his gaze fixed on the street ahead.

"You're making too much of that," he said, gripping the steering wheel as if he needed to concentrate on keeping it steady, though we were gliding along at twenty miles per hour. "She's just a friend."

"You don't touch your other friends," I pointed out. "You don't even hug them good-bye."

"Don't I? I think I do, sometimes."

"Well, I've never seen you. And I for sure haven't seen you touch anyone's leg like that except for mine."

"I couldn't be with her," Richard said, his gaze still leveled at the street. "She smokes. And I think she might drink too much. And she's too nervous, anyway, too high-strung."

At Richard's sunset party, standing in the kitchen after he's told me that he hasn't saved me any chicken, I simply say, "Oh," wishing I could magically erase Rebecca from the room. But even if I could accomplish that trick, it would be too late: Rebecca has already witnessed Richard's unenthused expression and words and tone, all directed at me. Now she is smiling, eyes half-closed, as if she is basking in the overhead light shining down from the kitchen ceiling. I would like to take two steps toward her, close my fist, and give her a quick rap on her skull. That would rouse her from her dreamy contentment!

"And you might as well not put together the food that you

brought," Richard continues, "since everyone is pretty much finished eating."

"Are you sure?" I ask, wondering if he's miffed that I didn't request the day off so that I could arrive at his party earlier. "It'll only take me a couple minutes to get it ready." In the bag I am carrying is homemade pesto and bread that I was planning to broil with mozzarella.

"I wouldn't bother," Richard answers. "People are finished eating, except for maybe dessert." He is leaning over the table in the kitchen. "Oh, I guess there is more chicken here," he says, opening a crumpled piece of foil. His voice is still offhand and without warmth. I move to the table and look down at a skimpy strip of gray breast, a piece so small it's been overlooked.

"*Richard,*" Rebecca says from the floor where she is camped out with her arms cozily twined around her youngest daughter. "I *love* your new house." She glances all around, her eyes brilliant and happy, and then smiles up at Richard. "It's just wonderful. I would *love* to live here."

I wish I had a rejoinder, something subtle yet stinging. But I can't think of anything, so I dump the measly piece of chicken onto a paper plate and walk with it into the living room, not wanting to hear any more of their exchange—not Rebecca's flirting voice, and, even less, the tone with which Richard might respond.

At the buffet table, I fill my plate, steering clear of desserts except for one chocolate truffle. I've gained eight pounds in the past year, since going back on the pill, which I did because Richard balked at using condoms and claimed he wasn't ready for a vasectomy. Recently, I've cut back on desserts in an attempt to lose the pounds I've gained, but I'm not going to give up chocolate or other sweets entirely, even if Richard does prefer skinny women. He said once, when I mentioned my slight weight gain, "You could eat fewer treats," his own chubby face averted. Remembering this, resentment rises hotly in me, along with anger at myself, for allowing him to get to me, even a little, over something so personal and petty. I nudge another chocolate truffle and a brownie onto my plate, thinking of how my dessert-loving women friends would cheer me if they were here. Then I push open the door and step outside.

Up ahead, small groups are gathered at the bluff near the lake. Richard began renting this lakefront cabin from a friend of mine at a discount after his caretaker arrangement ended. The cabin isn't nearly as close to Lake Michigan as the caretaker cottage was, and the master bedroom is in the windowless basement, so there's no bedside view at all; but still, it's on the lake, only a hundred yards back from the waves now rolling in.

At the edge of the bluff, I join a former teacher and long-time friend and chat with him as I eat my dinner and then invite him to walk with me on the beach. "Sure," Irving says. "I'd love to." I tell Richard, who is walking across the lawn with a bottle of wine in the fading light, that I am going for a walk with Irving, and I invite him to join us.

"I can't," he says. "I've got to stay here and host." I ask him if he wants me to stay and help him, and he says no.

Irving and I walk for a long time. I keep expecting him to suggest we turn back—he is fairly old, to my thinking, and he breathes as if he's not in the best shape. Twice I suggest that we can turn around if he likes, but I'm pleased when he answers, "No, let's keep walking."

The sun had begun to set as we started out; by the time we get back to the cottage, we've been gone for over an hour, and the beach is dark. Inside the cottage, though it is only a little past eight thirty, only a handful of guests remain. I'm glad to see that Rebecca isn't among them, but sorry for Richard's sake that his party has dwindled to just a few people so early in the evening.

Irving and I take seats on opposite sides of the room, and Irving begins conversing with the remaining partygoers in his usual articulate and witty fashion. Richard won't meet my eyes, and he won't even look in Irving's direction. Irving seems a little wickedly pleased. It occurs to me that sexuality isn't necessarily the only factor when it comes to jealousy, that Richard might be jealous of Irving's intellect or simply of our friendship.

Shortly after Irving and I return from the beach, all of the remaining guests say their good-byes and leave. I tell Richard I'm sorry for walking so long.

"It doesn't matter," Richard says.

"I expected the party would still be in full swing when I got back."

"I didn't think it would end so early, either."

We begin to clean up. Richard is still avoiding my eyes.

"You didn't mind my walking with Irving," I say. "Did you? You know he's never been anything but a friend to me."

"I know that," Richard says. "I didn't care."

We get ready for bed, and once we are lying down, I tell Richard that one of the reasons I walked for so long was that I hadn't wanted to watch him and Rebecca talking together, that I stayed out longer hoping that she would be gone by the time I returned.

"I've told you, she's not my type," Richard says, looking up at the ceiling. "I couldn't be serious about a smoker or someone so nervous."

⌐

MAYBE RICHARD WAS RIGHT in that he couldn't be serious about Rebecca, but I later learn that he becomes sexually involved with her, for several months. By then Richard has left me for a second time.

He first leaves me in early February, three months after the sunset party, without explanation, except for saying that he still loves me but he is not *in* love with me, and that he doesn't know why. He returns to me four months later, in June—for good, for forever, he says he is sure, he has made a mistake. He says that he's spent the past two weeks writing endlessly in his journal about the two of us, and that through all this instropection he has concluded that he wants to spend the rest of his life with me. "I've missed you so much. You ... and your family ... and ... and book club."

"Book club?" I ask.

"Yes, but mostly you—I'm so sorry for leaving you," he says. "What can I do to make up for it?"

We are standing at a counter in my kitchen. "You don't have to do anything," I say, turning fully toward him. "I'm just glad that you're back."

"But I feel I should do something. To make up for what I did to you."

A fragment of a fairy tale flits through my head, something about a suitor sent to find some golden apples before he's allowed to claim his bride. I smooth Richard's hair and smile at his worried face. His eyes seem so full of sorrow. I can hardly believe my luck. I feel as if I've returned from the dead, or as if Richard has. "We're back together," I say. "Neither of us has cancer. We have the rest of our lives. You don't have to do anything."

We begin to kiss, standing at the counter. Then I take Richard's hand, and he follows me into my bedroom. We lie down on my bed, and we hold each other and kiss some more. On the CD player in my living room, Lucinda Williams is singing, "You took my joy—I want it back / You took my joy—I want it back." By her sixth repetition, Richard is looking guilty. I consider getting up to change the music, but I decide that, rather than collecting golden apples, Richard can listen to these lyrics.

As we take off our clothes, Richard asks, "Are you sure you want to do this?"

"Yes. If you're sure you're back for good."

"I wouldn't be here if I wasn't," Richard says. "I've missed you so much."

I've stopped taking the pill, so we open a condom left from those we used during our first weeks together. Richard says that he still hates condoms, but it feels wonderful, anyway, to be back inside me again. I stroke his hair, his broad chest, his muscled arms. I can hardly believe that he has returned, that our plan of spending our lives together hasn't been lost.

Afterward, I invite Richard to stay for supper, although there isn't much food in the house. Richard seems awkward or shy but agrees to stay for the meal. I get up from the bed, feeling self-conscious about the small bulge of fat at my belly, wishing I had lost a little weight in the four months since I last saw him. I pull on a T-shirt and jeans, then go out to my garden and pick enough lettuce and radishes for a salad to accompany ham sandwiches.

Shortly after we've eaten, Richard leaves, saying that he'll call me the next day. Instead, the following morning, he writes me an e-mail: **I woke up feeling terrified. I can't believe this has happened. But I'm not going back on what I said to you**.

Two weeks of e-mails follow, during which we don't see each other or even talk on the phone. I'm patient at first, then angry, and then, afraid that I'm losing him again, patient and angry and hurt all at once. One evening I carry a large ceramic vase Richard gave me for my birthday out to the far reaches of my backyard and set it down in the high grass. I consider smashing it with a rock—but what if Richard returns, and we end up staying together? I will want this vase, filled with yellow and orange lilies, at the center of my dining room table as we share our summer dinners.

I leave the vase on the ground, near a stand of sassafras. If Richard returns, I'll return the vase to my house; if not, I'll leave it out in the yard, to crack and break over the winter. Back at my desk, I e-mail him, **We need to talk to each other in person**.

Getting together again won't do any good, Richard writes back. **Well, we tried. I'm very sorry that it didn't work.**

This e-mail arrrives just before I leave for Detroit to attend my parents' fiftieth wedding anniversary dinner. When I explain in a listless voice to my family what has happened, my youngest sister-in-law bristles. "Annie, why aren't you angry?" Sasha demands. "Why aren't you furious with him?"

"I guess I'm too sad to be angry," I answer.

My anger comes later—a hard, bitter core; a black, burning fire. One hot July evening I stalk to the edge of my yard, snatch up the heavy vase, and hurl it into my neighbor's pond. Satisfaction ripples through me—but it doesn't last. My sadness doesn't leave entirely until years later, when I marry a man who eclipses Richard and what he has done to me. And even then, the black fire, if I stir it, continues to burn. But eventually I realize that Richard wasn't so different from me. He was only trying to figure out and find love, and he made some mistakes along the way.

⁓

I BELIEVE RICHARD returned to me for that one evening because he was lonely, and he missed having sex with me, and probably at least for a few hours he believed that we would stay together. But I still don't fully understand why he left me in the first place. Maybe because I pressured him to be more assertive in his dealings with Beth, and, in the end, the most assertion he was able to muster was to say good-bye to me. Or perhaps it's that he had very little time between twenty years of fidelity to his wife and our relationship, and he wasn't ready yet to commit to just one woman again. And maybe even the few pounds I gained after going on the pill influenced him to some degree. But whatever the causes or reasons for Richard's decision, in retrospect, I could have seen the end sooner.

I could have seen it on a November evening several weeks after the sunset party, when I drove up to my friend's cabin that Richard was renting. Richard was expecting me, but he didn't notice me arriving. It was dark out, and I saw him through the lighted windows, dancing by himself in the kitchen. His arms were raised, cocked at right angles, fists striking the air around his head in time to the music, which I couldn't hear. His eyes were closed, and on his face was a joyous smile. Although I could only see him from the waist up, I could tell that his pelvis was grinding.

His look as he danced reminded me of when we were in

Colorado, how the color returned to his face and the liveliness to his eyes when we came down out of the mountains. But this time what Richard felt had nothing to do with me. I hadn't seen such exuberance coming from him in months while I was in his presence.

When I entered the cabin, Richard stopped dancing.

"Don't stop," I said. "C'mon, I'll dance with you."

Richard smoothed his hands over his shirt and shook his head.

"But you looked so happy, dancing just now."

"Did I?" Richard answered, his voice flat. He looked at me but didn't smile. The glint from his eyes was gone, as it was when he was starving for oxygen. But he was breathing fine.

"C'mon," I pleaded. I held out my hands.

"No," Richard said. "I don't feel like it anymore."

"But you looked so happy," I said again.

His hands stayed limp at his sides, his feet remained still. Without meeting my eyes, Richard said, "I'm all done."

Flames

THE RINGING PHONE reaches through the black caul of my sleep. My eyes open on red numbers—1:20 A.M.—and I leap out of bed and stumble into the kitchen. As I pick up the handset, I am fully awake.

"Mom? Are you there?"

"Marly, what's wrong?"

"Mitch came home from the bar and I wouldn't let him in and he kicked down the door."

I ask if she's okay, and she says that she is. I flip on the light and ask where she is now.

"I'm still here ... in my apartment ... waiting for the police."

"Where's Mitch?" Standing in my big kitchen, I look around me for a weapon, as if I could snatch it up and hand it through the phone line.

"He went up to the third floor, to Jared's apartment, I think."

"What happened? Did he hurt you?"

"Not really," Marly says. "He pushed me and he was shouting. I told him I'd called the police, so then he stormed upstairs."

"Why did you lock him out?"

Marly's voice rises to a higher note. "He said he was going out to the bar. I *asked* him not to. I *told him* he couldn't go to the bar and then come back here. I told him that if he came back here drunk, I wasn't going to let him in." Beneath the surface distress and frustration in Marly's voice, I hear fear held in check, and all at once I know she is holding something back: Mitch has come home drunk before tonight and mistreated her. He has hit her, or forced sex on her, or abused her in some other way, and probably on more than one occasion.

Across my kitchen, on my butcher block, are my knives of various sizes, plus a twelve-inch sharpening steel with a heavy wooden handle. I shrink from the idea of thrusting a knife into a man's chest, but I easily picture picking up the steel and bludgeoning Mitch with it.

"Do you have something you can use for a weapon?" I ask. "In case he comes back?"

"I don't know, let me think."

"What about your pepper spray?" I bought Marly a canister, along with one for myself, after a man flashed me at the state park.

"I don't have it anymore," Marly says. "I gave it to a friend."

I tell her to go get her sharpening steel and to hide all her sharp knives at the back of a drawer and to keep the steel in her hand. I listen to her moving about, and then she says, "Okay, I've got the steel."

"Did you hide the knives?"

A drawer squawks. "I'm doing that now."

"What about the door to your apartment? Can you push it back into place?"

Marly says it's not even a real door—just a piece of paneling left over from when they paneled the lobby, with a now useless deadbolt and chain attached—but she has leaned it across the opening to keep the cats from running out. I tell her to push the heaviest piece of furniture she can move up against it, and she says she has already pushed her big bookcase there.

"Okay, good. Keep your eye on the door while we're talking, and don't let go of the steel. If he comes back, tell him that you have a weapon and that he better stay out. And if he comes in, don't wait for him to attack first—hit him over the head, as hard as you can. And don't stop hitting until he leaves or stops moving."

It feels unreal to be standing in my kitchen at one thirty in the morning and talking on the phone like this with my daughter, even though I've been through something similar with a friend whose ex-husband broke down her door twice. I wonder if I should hang up and jump in my car and race up to Grand Rapids; but it's a forty-five minute drive from my house, and I'm afraid that, after I hang up, something else bad might happen. It makes more sense to stay on the line and talk with Marly and help her figure out what to do. If Mitch comes back downstairs and attacks Marly while we are talking, I can hang up and call 9-1-1 and tell them that Marly is in immediate danger. I try not to think of the worst-case scenario: that Marly might be murdered as I am standing in my kitchen, while I listen to her cries through the phone.

If I had a husband, or a boyfriend, he could be driving up to Marly's apartment while I talk with her. I can't call Marly's dad for help—Ray is living in California with his second wife. And I can't call Richard, whom I haven't seen since last month, when I told him, after he left me for the second time, that I wanted no more contact with him. And anyway, Richard always shrank from any kind of confrontation. I consider my father and my four brothers with a yearning sadness—they all live too far away to come to our aid. If I had a cell phone, I could be driving to Grand Rapids right now, drawing closer to Marly every moment and talking with her at the same time. But maybe rather than my going there, the best plan is for Marly to leave her apartment and drive to my house.

"Marly, I'm thinking you should just come down here."

"I can't. I have to wait for the police so I can tell them what happened and where Mitch is now."

"Can't the apartment manager do that?"

"I called Kirk, but he didn't answer. He never answers his phone."

"Did the police say how soon they'd get there?"

"No. But Wendell should be here soon. Before I called you, I called Wendell. He's working till two, and he said he'd come over the minute he gets off."

"Oh, good," I say. We've known Wendell for years—he's the older brother of one of Marly's friends from grade school. Wendell goes to Grand Valley State University during the week and tends bar in Grand Rapids on weekend nights.

A year or so ago, I suggested that Marly date Wendell instead of just being his friend. Wendell is sweet, smart, engaging, and levelheaded. Marly had smiled fondly when I spoke

Wendell's name and narrowed her eyes as if picturing him. "He looks like a Hobbit," she said.

"He does not," I protested. "He's not very tall and he's not super handsome, but he doesn't look like a Hobbit."

Marly had continued to smile with both affection and discernment. "Like Frodo," she said.

"Marly, you pick your boyfriends by looks too much, I think."

"Oh, like you don't? Not that I think your boyfriends look hot, *at all*, but *you* do—even that dorky bald guy with that terrible mullet."

"Okay, fine," I said. "Only date guys you think are really hot. But make sure they're good guys, too."

"Good guys, bad guys," Marly answered in a dreary singsong, as if she were bored with the subject.

"What do you mean, Marly?"

She had hesitated. Then she said, "It's not so easy to tell all the time."

Thinking back to her words and her tone, I can hear the danger hidden in them. Mitch had been living with Marly then for about a year. He had lavished attention on her at first, calling her "honey" and "darlin'" and "baby" at every turn, gazing at her with what seemed to me false adoration. Marly gazed back as if hoping to believe him. Her boyfriend before Mitch was wholly undemonstrative, emotionally flat. Rico and Marly had lived together for fourteen months, but Rico never said that he loved her. Marly was lured away from Rico by Mitch, who told Marly he loved her almost as soon as they met. But Mitch's initial lavish attention soon became sporadic, and everything else about him has turned out to be sporadic, too, including looking for work, going to work when he has a job, and helping out around the house. During the past year, Marly has asked Mitch to leave, again and again. But he says he doesn't have anywhere else to go.

Other than the attention he first paid her, I've never seen what Marly saw in Mitch. He has no evident ambitions, other than to someday buy another motorcycle, he drinks a lot and smokes, and he isn't even much to look at: small and wiry in an unhealthy way—wizened, almost, like an old man, although he claims he is only twenty-eight. He looks more like thirty-five, and his facial features make me think of a gnome. He has seemed pitiful to me, but not dangerous until now.

I ask Marly if she is keeping an eye on her doorway, and she says that she is.

"And you still have the steel in your hand?"

"Yes."

"I just want you to be ready, in case he comes back."

"I know. I will be."

Marly and I continue to talk. I wish, but keep to myself, that she had barred Mitch in a less confrontational way, that she had locked him out in the daytime and when he wasn't drunk, and that she had done it with someone there to back her up: a male friend or the apartment manager or even me. I look across the kitchen at the clock. It is ten after two. "I wonder if I should have just driven up," I say. "I'd be there by now."

"Quiet, Mom," Marly warns. "Someone's at the door."

My breath seems to stop. I strain my ears for Mitch. Should I hang up, dial 9-1-1? But I can't make myself cut my connection to my child.

I hear a voice say, "Are you Marly?"

"Mom, the police are here," Marly says. "I'll call you back."

I ask her to call me right away, and she says okay, and then the phone goes silent.

I wander numbly around my kitchen. It is two twenty-five, and I'm scheduled to work the morning shift. I wonder if I should drive to Grand Rapids, spend the night with Marly, call the bus company, and leave a message that I can't make it in. They can get by with just two drivers in the morning. But Wendell is due to arrive at Marly's apartment any minute, and he is either going to stay with her there, or take her somewhere else. I'm not sure what I should do. Maybe I'm only hesitating to race up to Grand Rapids because it's forty-five minutes away and it's late and I'm tired and I'm supposed to be at my job in four hours.

I decide I better get ready to drive up to Marly's apartment. Since I might not have a chance to shower in the morning, I take off the T-shirt I went to bed in, lean over the bathroom sink, and wash my armpits. In my bedroom, I change my underwear, pull on a fresh T-shirt and my jeans and socks and shoes. Then I wander back out to the kitchen and stop beside my largest plant, whose leaves and vines spill down in lavish waves from the sink island to the floor. Most of the philodendron's leaves are pure green or green spattered with flecks of pale yellow and white, but one leaf near the top has a wide, triangular stripe of creamy white running through it, and for some reason it always lifts my spirits to rest my gaze on that rich, creamy triangle bordered by deep green.

I rub some of the dust from the white-striped leaf and see that all the leaves need to be wiped clean with a wet cloth: another chore I will never get around to, like sorting through my closets and steam-cleaning my carpets. As I finger the leaf, my thoughts stray to Richard: even though his second departure has left me still feeling, after a month, as if a hole has been torn in my chest, it's nothing compared to how I will feel if Marly is taken from me. Losing my first child right after her birth is the hardest thing I've ever had to get used to; losing the only child I have left, after loving her all these years, would be more than I can take. I would murder Mitch. I would beat him to death with a baseball bat, even though I know that wouldn't really help.

Too tired to keep standing up or to pace, I pull out a kitchen chair and sit back down at my oak table. The phone rings again. I click it on and breathe in at the sound of my daughter's voice. The police have left, Marly tells me. They were there for only fifteen minutes. She sounds more frustrated than frightened. "They told me I have no right to lock him out because he lives here, too."

"What? Even though he's paying no rent and you've told him to leave?"

"They say that doesn't matter, that because he lives here, he has a right to come in, even if he has to break down the door."

"So, once you let someone live with you, you're stuck with him for good?"

"Apparently," Marly says.

"That's crazy."

"They say if he is violent, I can get a personal protection order, but until I have one, they can't do anything."

I ask her if the police at least went upstairs to Jared's apartment to have a talk with Mitch, and Marly says, no, they didn't, and now Mitch is up there getting drunker. I ask her how she knows this, and she says that Jared walked into the lobby while she was talking with the police, carrying a case of beer, and he walked right past the police and up the stairs. "And Mom," Marly says, "the police were really shitty to me.

They acted like I was the one who had caused all the trouble. And one of them said something really, really crappy. He said, 'Is this the first time you've called to report your boyfriend?' I said, 'Yes.' And he sneered at me and said, 'Well, it won't be the last time.' And the other one just stood there looking at me as if I were dirt."

"They have no right to act like that," I say. "They have no business talking and acting like that to anyone! What a couple of jerks. Did they at least help you fix the door?"

"No. They just strutted around with their guns and holsters like they were bored and had more important things to do."

"I thought police were being trained about how to deal with domestic violence."

"Evidently not in Grand Rapids."

I glance around at my quiet, empty kitchen. "Marly, why don't you come down here tonight?"

But she doesn't want to leave her cats, who can get around the door if they try, and anyway, she says, my house is no safer than hers, what with its puny locks and being way out in the country. Besides, Wendell should get there any minute, and he can help her rig up the door.

We continue to wait together on the phone. A few minutes later Marly lets out a happy cry: "Wendell's here!"

I hear them greeting each other. Then Marly says again, more quietly, "Wendell's here, Mom."

"Good! Can I speak to him?"

Marly hands the phone to Wendell, and I say hi to him and thank him for coming over.

"It's no problem," he says. "I'm glad to do it."

I ask him if he can spend the rest of the night with Marly, and he says sure, he plans on it.

"And if you leave, you'll take her with you?"

"Yes," Wendell says cheerfully.

"And if you stay, will you be able to fix the door?"

"We'll patch it up somehow," Wendell says. "I brought some tools from the bar."

"Oh, great. And you're going to stay there all night, or else take Marly with you?" I say, aware that I'm not sounding normal, that I've asked Wendell this already.

"Yes, I will," Wendell says cheerfully and patiently. "Don't worry, I won't leave her by herself."

I thank Wendell again and talk to Marly a little longer. She says they are going to stay at her apartment—she's afraid that if she leaves, Mitch will come back and trash all her stuff. I make her promise to call me if they decide to go somewhere else, so that I'll know where she is in case something else happens.

After Marly hangs up, I take off my jeans and my shoes and lie back down on my bed. But I'm unable to sleep. What if Mitch returns, reinforced by more beer and maybe a weapon, and murders them both? Maybe he already did, shortly after I hung up the phone. I won't find out if that has happened until I hear from one of Marly's neighbors or those worthless police.

Curled up on my side with my eyes closed, I can't help wondering what I might have done wrong in raising Marly for her to reach this point. Maybe if her father and I had stayed together, or I hadn't had so many boyfriends, she would now be in a healthier relationship. I've kept much of my love life to myself, and I've only once let a man spend the night when Marly was with me, but children know more than you tell them, more than you allow them to see. Still, while I've made some bad choices, I've made no really dangerous ones. I've never been physically harmed. Yet Richard's breaking up with me a second time knocked the wind out of my spirit and hurt as much as being beaten; it left my chest aching so much that it hurt to breathe. But whatever Mitch has done to Marly is surely worse. My mind approaches and then skitters away from what Mitch might have done to make Marly lock him out.

I rearrange my blankets and pillows again and settle back in and pray for Marly's safety, even though I don't believe that praying really works. Why should my prayers be answered, when so many mothers are forced to live with the suffering and even the deaths of their children? I wouldn't be the first mother to lose more than one child. Finally drowsiness overcomes me, and I fall into a deep but agitated sleep full of vivid, disjointed dreams.

MARLY CALLS ME at six, sounding cheerful. She is in a van with Wendell and also Amelia, a friend of Marly's who has a black belt in karate. They are driving across town to Amelia's apartment with Marly's cats, her camera, her photographs, her computer, and, as Marly phrases it, "anything and everything else of sentimental value." Marly tells me that Mitch came back at four in the morning and broke down the door again, but when he saw Wendell, he retreated upstairs, and Wendell once again repatched and replaced the door.

Marly spends the next two nights across town at her friend Amelia's apartment. On the third day, she starts off for Chicago, where her dad's parents live. She has been planning for some time to fly out to California to spend a week with her dad, first staying one night with her grandparents, who will drive her to O'Hare. But as Marly is heading for Chicago, driving south on 196, she calls me.

"Mom, my car is acting really funny."

"What's it doing?"

"It's shaking, a lot."

"What part of it is shaking?"

"All of it. It's shimmying like crazy. It wasn't too bad at first, but in the last ten minutes, it's gotten way worse."

"Well, you better not drive it to Chicago," I say. "Where are you now?"

"On the expressway north of Saugatuck."

"You better swing by here, and take my car."

"Are you sure? The engine seems okay, it's just the body."

I tell her to leave her car with me, and I'll take it in to work and have our bus mechanic check it over. Twenty minutes later, Marly pulls her gold hatchback into my driveway. As she gets out of her car, her bright, unnaturally red hair strikes me as too noticeable, too easy to spot. She's been dying her hair fire-engine red ever since she was sixteen, and for the first time I fear that it's not a safe color. Backlit by the sun, the tips of her hair glow like flames, as if her head is edged with fire. I want to suggest she wear a hood, or re-dye her hair a dull brown. But I think I'm likely over-worrying, and I don't want to scare her further, so I don't say anything.

I haven't seen Marly since Mitch broke down her door, so I'm even gladder than usual for the chance to wrap my arms around her slender shoulders. As I rub her bare arm with my fingers and look at her face, I wonder, as I have many times before, if my desire to touch her skin and feel her warmth and see her open eyes is stronger in me because I held my other child only once, after her body was cold, and I only ever saw her with her eyes closed.

I send Marly off to Chicago in my white Accord and drive

her gold Civic in to work. Luckily it's only a five-minute drive—
the car feels as if it might shake apart. Phil, the bus company's
mechanic, says he'll take it for a spin while I'm out picking up
passengers, and when I come back later for a break and ask
him if he's found out what is wrong, Phil says, "The lug nuts
on both front tires were loose. Some were so loose, I could
turn them with my hand." Phil is a laid-back, peaceful hippie,
almost impossible to rattle, but now he looks grave and more
alert than usual. With the clean back of his greasy hand, he
wipes the sweat from his brow. We are standing in the parking
lot outside the bus garage.

"Could those lug nuts have come loose on their own?" I
ask him. "Or did someone loosen them on purpose?"

"Who would loosen them on purpose?" Phil asks, squinting against the sun.

"Marly's ex-boyfriend," I say. "She locked him out of her
apartment a few nights ago, and he broke down the door three
times after that." According to Marly's apartment mates, Mitch
had entered a third time, after Marly was gone, by splintering
the door with a crowbar.

"Jeez," Phil says. "Some guys have a hard time taking a
hint they're not wanted."

I smile sourly and tell Phil that, even though the manager
finally kicked Mitch out of the building, he lurked around outside for the next few days, and during that entire time—for two
days and two nights—Marly's car was parked in the untended
lot next door.

Phil looks down at the ground and shakes his head.

"He could have killed her," I say, "if those wheels had
come off at seventy miles an hour! That's probably what he
was hoping for, the little bastard."

"Well, they could have come loose on their own, too," Phil says. He asks if Marly has had any work done on her car lately, and I tell him that Mitch replaced the brakes a few months back.

"That's probably what happened," Phil says. "You said he's a little guy, right? He probably didn't have the strength to tighten the nuts all the way, and they slowly worked themselves loose."

"He's bigger than me," I say, "and I've changed several tires on that car, and the nuts have never come loose."

Phil shrugs. "Maybe he wasn't as conscientious as you about getting them tight again. But anyway, I tightened them up good."

I thank Phil. Then I say, "But don't you think I should report this to the police? Marly could have been killed."

"She could have," Phil agrees. He looks up the street, toward the highway overpass, under which cars are thundering. "If she'd kept driving that car for much longer, the wheels would have disengaged. Not a good thing to happen when you're barreling down the expressway." But, Phil reiterates, Mitch didn't necessarily do anything wrong on purpose, and even if he did, it couldn't be proved, since his fingerprints could still be on the car from the brake job he had done.

That night, I call Marly's dad and tell him about her car. Ray insists that Marly should not return to Michigan, that she should stay in California, at least for a while; she can get a job for the remaining two months of summer, and then go to college in nearby Arcata in the fall.

But Marly has an interview for a receptionist job at Planned Parenthood in Grand Rapids lined up for next week, and she doesn't want to pass up that opportunity. "And besides," she tells me over the phone, "I'd feel really bad if I let Mitch drive me out of my apartment." I agree with Ray that if staying a couple of thousand miles away is necessary to keep Marly safe, then that is obviously what she should do. But it's impossible to know how much precaution is needed.

⌒

DURING THE WEEK Marly is away, I half-consider, half-fantasize about borrowing a gun from one of my hunter neighbors, learning to use it, and driving up to Grand Rapids and murdering Mitch. Maybe a feminist lawyer would take my case, and I'd go free, and if I did end up in prison, at least I'd have a lot of time to read. But I'd miss going for walks by the river and the lake, and I would hate being bossed or harassed by guards or other inmates. And I don't really believe I have a right to kill Mitch, unless he murders Marly or hurts her badly.

Instead of borrowing a gun, I buy a cell phone; while it's not much of an action, it seems better than doing nothing at all. Now, when Marly returns from visiting her dad, she can reach me wherever I am, twenty-four hours a day. If she needs my help suddenly, I'll drop everything and race up to her while keeping her on the line.

Although I miss her, I dread Marly's return from California. When I close my eyes at night, I see Marly's gold hatchback hurtling down the expressway, its wheels flying off, the car skidding on its axles. Although Marly's car is once again safe, a man who could demolish her apartment door and sabotage her car is capable of further endangerment. One day while I'm out buying groceries, I stop in a sporting goods store and buy two canisters of pepper spray, one to replace my old, unused canister and the other to replace the one Marly has given away. And on the morning after Marly returns from visiting her dad, we drive from my house, each in our own car because we'll go our separate ways later, to meet for a consultation at the Center for Women in Transition.

The legal aide on duty, a blond woman in her late twenties, is a lawyer who volunteers at the center. She leads us to a conference room with a long table and closes the door behind us. Marly and I pull out chairs and take seats side by side. The lawyer, who introduces herself as Teresa, sits at the table's head and begins to ask Marly about Mitch and why she wants a personal protection order against him. Marly tells her about the incident with the door. Teresa asks, "And besides the door, were there other incidents?"

"Um, what do you mean?" Marly says. She is turned toward Teresa, sitting with her back slanted at me.

"Was Mitch abusive in other ways?" Teresa asks. She clicks her pen and waits, but Marly keeps quiet. "For instance, did he call you names, or make threats?"

Marly drops her gaze and her voice. "Not names," she says. "But he's made threats. He's said some really terrible things. Sometimes he would say something so awful that I couldn't really believe it. It was like something out of a gangster movie. I'd tell myself that I must have heard him wrong, because people didn't talk like that in real life."

"Can you remember what he said?" Teresa asks. She clicks her pen again and waits. Marly sits with her shoulders tense and hunched and her face half-turned away from me. Her bright-red hair, newly cut, makes her neck look pale and fragile.

"I know it's hard to talk about," Teresa says, "but the judge is going to want to know the details. You won't have to repeat any of this in court. I'm just taking a few notes, and then I'll help you fill out the request, and you'll take it to the court and the judge will read it and make his decision. Does that sound okay?"

"Yes," Marly says. But she continues to look down at the table as if waiting for something.

Finally it occurs to me that she doesn't want me to hear her answers. "I'm going to go find a bathroom," I say, and I push back my chair and stand.

"Okay," Marly says brightly, sitting up a little, her shoulders lifting.

I leave the room, closing the door behind me. I find a bathroom and use it even though I don't really need to and then wander the center's halls. T-shirts of bright yellow, pink, lavender, white, and blue are pinned to the walls all along one hallway, each with a different woman's name hand-painted on it: **Sharon**, **Ashley**, and **Cathy**; **Maria**, **Katie**, and **Pam**; **Jessica** and **Christine**. In smaller writing, around the women's names, are handwritten messages: "**a wonderful mother**," "**my dearest daughter**," "**we love you**," "**she will be missed forever**." At the end of the line of T-shirts is a poster with an explanation: the names on the T-shirts are the names of local women who have been abused and killed by their husbands and ex-husbands, their boyfriends and ex-boyfriends. These T-shirts, the poster further explains, have been made by the children, mothers, sisters, and friends of the battered and murdered women. At the bottom of the poster is a list of statistics: **Domestic violence is the number one cause of injury to women in the U.S. One in three women are battered at some time in their lives. Four thousand American women are killed by their partners every year.**

I turn away from this hallway and make my way back to the conference room, stopping a few feet from the door so that

I can look in through its window without being seen. Marly is talking, and Teresa is listening intently, a yellow legal pad with a few scribbled notes before her. I fade back from the conference room door, walk down the hall in the opposite direction, and stop before another wall poster that reads in big purple letters: **NO ONE DESERVES TO BE SEXUALLY ASSAULTED**, and underneath, in smaller, black letters: **HELP AND SUPPORT ARE AVAILABLE**. Below this is a list of common reactions to rape: **fear, anxiety, shock, disbelief, helplessness, depression, anger, shame, embarrassment, self-blame, guilt, flashbacks, and isolation.** I read the rest of the poster, then return again to within a few feet of the window that looks into the conference room. Teresa is still sitting quietly, but her legal pad has been pushed aside. Marly is bent over a form composed of two pieces of paper joined at the center. She is writing quickly, words flowing from her pen. As I watch, she flips the double sheet over, which is filled with her tiny handwriting, and continues on the backside.

I fade back from the conference room door, and this time I wander the halls without looking at or reading what is on them, fretting and fuming, trying to not think of what Mitch might have done to my child. Maybe I should kill Mitch, rather than wait to see if the personal protection order will work. It's just a piece of paper. A lot of men ignore PPOs and continue to abuse and eventually murder their girlfriends and wives. Why should I wait to see whether Mitch will obey the order and stay away from Marly? Why should I give him another chance to do her harm? Marly's apartment mates didn't see Mitch during the week Marly was in California, and Marly has not seen or talked with him since the night she locked him out, but after Marly returns to her apartment, Mitch might show up again.

When I return to the conference room for a third time, Marly is still writing, but nearing the end of the fourth and last page of the document. I open the door and take the seat beside her, and she writes to the end of the page. "I'm done," she announces, to Teresa and to me, it seems, as well as to herself.

I glance over at the form and her shaking hand. "Is this what you'll give the judge?" I ask.

"Yes," Marly tells me.

"Do you want me to read it?" I ask, thinking I can edit it, if it needs it—Marly is a terrible speller, and I want the judge to see her story clearly and to rule in her favor.

"No," Marly says.

"Are you sure?" I press, leaning forward, not quite reaching out my hand. I also want to know what has happened to Marly, if she wants me to.

"Yes, I'm sure," Marly says. "There's no reason for you to see this."

"Okay," I murmur, folding my arms across my breasts, sitting back in my chair.

When Marly was three and six and ten and I would coddle her or hover, my father would admonish me: "When are you going to cut the cord?" My mom would defend me and, at the same time, gently tease me: "She's cutting it. A little at a time." At the Center for Women in Transition, we've reached another of those times. Is it harder for me to sit back and do nothing because right after my first child's cord was cut, I was involuntarily sedated, and by the time I regained consciousness, she had died? But wouldn't any mother, not just those who have already lost one daughter, string whole nets of cords around their girls to ensure their safety? Except no cords or nets are strong enough, and nothing and no one can be ensured.

Marly hands the form filled with her tiny handwriting to Teresa, who reads through the pages quickly, her eyes flickering, her lips thinning and tightening. When Teresa comes to the end of the statement, she looks up, her face grim. "You won't have any problem," she says. "The judge will grant you the order. Without question."

We thank her, and I make out a donation check, and then we set off in our two cars for the Ottawa County Courthouse, which, according to Teresa, processes PPOs in a matter of hours, whereas the courthouse in Kent County, which encompasses Grand Rapids, can take as long as a week.

We park in a lot in downtown Grand Haven, a block from the courthouse, and Marly and I get out of our cars and walk toward the tall, old formal building. It's a hot and gritty summer day, and as we stride down the street, squinting against the wind, I scan the other pedestrians and the passengers and drivers of the passing cars for Mitch's face, my hand lightly gripping the canister of pepper spray in my pocket. Mitch can't know we are here—Grand Haven is thirty or so miles from Grand Rapids and Mitch doesn't know that we are about to process an order against him—but since we don't know where he is, it's easy to imagine him being anywhere, including on the same street where we are walking.

Just inside the courthouse door, a stern black woman sitting at the security desk asks us if we are carrying any weapons, and she rattles through a list that includes knives, guns, razor blades, pepper spray, ammunition, and explosives.

"Well, I have pepper spray," I say.

"You do? You're carrying it?" she asks, her eyes widened in disbelief.

"It's in my pocket," I say.

"Set it on the desk," she orders, and in one motion, Marly and I each pull our pepper spray canisters out of our pockets and set them down in front of the woman. Lines above her eyes and around her mouth leap out sharply. "What are you doing, bringing those in here?" she asks loudly. Marly and I stare at her without responding. "What are you here for?" the woman demands, her voice echoing up and down the high-ceilinged hall.

I answer her quietly: "To get a personal protection order for my daughter."

The woman looks between our two faces, and her own face softens. "Well, you can't bring those in here," she says, her voice lowered. "It's illegal. Go take them back to your car, and then you can come in."

Marly and I scoop up the canisters and return them to our pockets. Outside, walking toward the parking lot, we are smiling a little. It all seems so odd and unreal. The chances of our being attacked on this busy downtown street on a bright summer morning seem incalculably small. Yet on the short walk back to the courthouse, I feel unsafe without my pepper spray in my pocket and my hand closed around it, my thumb ready to press the nozzle.

The judge we need to see is in session, so we leave the form with his receptionist, who says the judge will look at it during his next break, and when we return from strolling the waxed, echoing halls a half hour later, the personal protection order is signed and ready to be delivered.

We leave the courthouse, and Marly heads back to Grand Rapids, to her apartment, while I drive back to my house. I had pushed for Marly to stay with me at least until the PPO was delivered, but she insisted that she was likely safer at her own apartment, since Kirk has replaced the splintered piece of paneling with a standard, solid door complete with a heavy chain and dead bolt, and Amelia, Marly's black-belt friend, is going to stay with Marly the next few nights. One of Marly's apartment mates has found out where Mitch is staying, and Wendell and Amelia plan to show up there this afternoon, knock on the door, and hand him the PPO.

Marly calls me in the evening. "Wendell and Amelia delivered the PPO," she says. "Mitch started to read it. Then he crumpled it up and threw it on the ground. But that doesn't matter—as long as he touches it with his hand, it's considered served."

"But if he's angry, Marly . . . What if he comes looking for you?"

"Wendell and Amelia are here with me. And, like you say, Mitch is a coward. Plus, he really hated that time he spent in jail, and he's afraid of being put back in."

"He was in jail before?"

"Yeah, I told you. About ten years ago, for vagrancy, in Texas."

Two more days pass, without incident or news of Mitch. Then Marly hears that Mitch has gone to live with his sister in Lubbock, that she sent him money for a one-way bus ticket, and he left for Texas that same day.

⌒

MARLY INTERVIEWS for the receptionist job at Planned Parenthood along with over a hundred other applicants. She knows it's a long shot, given the tight job market and her minimal experience, and she isn't too disappointed when she finds out that she hasn't been hired. For the past three years, off and on, she's been taking core classes and photography at Grand Rapids Community College, and although she loves photography, from the start she has been adamant about not wanting to rely on it for her bread and butter. "I just want to take photos of whatever I feel like," she has said more than once, "not perfect slices of strawberry shortcake, or women in their god-awful bridesmaids dresses." But recently, she's begun to consider photography of a different sort, and after she's passed over for the job at Planned Parenthood, she makes up her mind: she will become an X-ray technician; she will take pictures of people's bones for a living. And maybe, on the side, she'll combine X-ray technology with conventional photography to produce a new kind of art.

Marly starts searching online for programs close to Grand Rapids. One evening I'm checking the course listings of a college that has just opened near my house to see if they offer an X-ray tech degree when my eye stops on another course of study: veterinary technician. I think of all the pets and strays Marly has cared for over the years: the dozen or more cats; the baby bunnies, Uno and Dos; and the days-old baby possum. Her childhood love for animals has not abated, and the next time I speak with her, I mention the possibility of her becoming a vet tech.

"That's it!" Marly cries. "That's exactly it!" She investigates various programs, arranges for her school records to be transferred, and has her name placed on the waiting list of a vet tech program in Muskegon. Meanwhile, she finds another temp filing job and begins volunteering at an animal shelter.

One day I call her, as usual. "I helped adopt out another

kitten today," Marly says. "A real sweet little boy, all gray. And that skittish orange girl who was found stinking of lighter fluid, with her face and body singed? She's beginning to warm up. She really surprised me today. I was petting her, and she closed her eyes and leaned right into my hand." Marly says that she and the other shelter workers are still looking for a name for the young orange cat that was doused with lighter fluid and, they suspect, intentionally set on fire. "I'd like to call her Flame," Marly says. "Partly because of her color but mainly because of what happened to her. And we're also considering Phoenix, and Baptism by Fire." They've come up with other names, unrelated to the cat's appearance or her circumstances, but none of them have stuck so far.

Marly and I chat on the phone a little longer. As we are hanging up Marly says, "So, Mom, how long are you going to keep calling me every day?" There is a smile in her voice, as well as a challenge. About a month has passed since she phoned me at 1:20 in the morning.

"I don't know," I say. "I guess I can stop."

"You can keep calling me every day, if you want," Marly says. "It's up to you. But you can quit worrying now."

We say good-bye, and I set down the phone. Wandering around my kitchen, I remind myself to not dwell on Marly's splintered door, or the loosened lug nuts of her car, or the T-shirts at the center painted with the names of battered and murdered women. Instead, I think of the young orange cat that was set on fire but is now recovering. And I think of her potential names: Baptism by Fire, Phoenix, Flame. And in my mind I see Marly, surrounded by fire yet unsinged. Not Marly as she is now, with her mane of flaming hair, but when she was just born: red-faced, wailing in protest, already struggling, already strong; twisting and kicking in the doctor's grasp even before the cord was cut; unlike her quiet sister, ready to take on the world.

Strange Love

THE FIRST TIME I SEE HAL, he is approaching from the distance, walking north along the shoreline as I am walking south. It's the first week of October, and the weather has turned chilly. Dusk is just beginning to soften the blue sky and, except for us, the beach is deserted. *Could I take him out?* I wonder. I mean beat him up, not date him. Over a year has passed since I was flashed on a beach several miles north of here, and nearly a decade has passed since a friend of a friend was raped on this very beach, one October; still, with a needling of dread, I realize that it's getting dark and I've left my pepper spray in my car.

As the man gradually draws nearer, I size him up. He is tall and, although slender, wide-shouldered. I regret that I am only five feet four. Well, I'll look invulnerable. Tough. Not-to-be-messed-with.

He is wearing a navy-blue baseball cap and a long-sleeved windbreaker. His jeans are rolled up, and, to my surprise, he is barefoot and walking with his feet in the cold water. As he draws closer, I relax a little, and when we are near enough to speak, he says hi. I answer hello. As he passes by me I realize that all my fear has evaporated.

When I reach my usual place to stop—a big, flat, pink quartz rock with several thick, creamy stripes—I gaze out at the rows of breaking waves. I often gaze at the lake's vast, shifting surface to help me sort through my thoughts, but now I take it in only briefly, admiring its beauty and power. Then I turn and begin walking back up the beach. The man also has turned around, somewhere to the north. This time as we approach each other, I feel an urge to speak; seeing him warmly dressed but wading in the cold water, I want to tell him that I went swimming just a few days ago.

I swam out into Lake Michigan almost daily all summer, not stopping at the second sandbar but stroking farther and farther outward, until the lake lay all around me in a wide, welcoming circle. I swam out for exercise and for my love of the lake and for the feel of the water, and because this lake is where my first baby's ashes were scattered, but this summer I swam out farther and more often than usual because it helped to release my anger at Richard's desertion. I didn't think about Mitch, my daughter's awful ex-boyfriend; when I heard that Mitch had taken off for Texas, I pretty much put him out of my mind. I was not able to so easily erase Richard, who was still in the vicinity, but the farther out I swam, it seemed, the farther I left him behind. The lake dwarfed Richard and his puny though painful actions. The lake reminded me that the world was beautiful and large.

Autumn's cooler weather put an end to these swims, but three days ago the air turned unseasonably warm, and I braved the cold water one last time. While swimming out on my back, looking up at the sky, three gulls flew over me with their beaks opened, crying down at me, the sky beyond them a deep, blue dome. Afterward, I had to blast my car's heater to drive the chill from my bones, but I'm still feeling pleased with my last, late-season swim, and I want to boast about it to this stranger who is gradually wading toward me.

When we are within speaking distance, I gesture at his feet and say, "You're not going to be able to do that much longer."

He slows his steps and says, "The water is actually warmer than the air right now."

"I went swimming on Monday," I brag, smiling as I pass him by.

He answers, "I went swimming today."

I stop short and face him. "*Today?*"

"In a wet suit," he explains.

My heart leaps at this new possibility—extra days in the lake that I might gain. "I never thought of using a wet suit to extend the season."

"I use it for snorkeling, too," the man says, smiling, nodding his head as if he is agreeing with himself. "I went snorkeling today."

"Really? You snorkel out there? What's there to see?"

"Rock formations. Fish. Lines etched into the lake bottom by the movement of the water."

I ask him more questions, wanting to make sure that I learn enough to buy and use a wet suit on my own. I'm not yet thinking about dating him. He is clean-cut and good-looking, and I figure that he's married—he seems too good a catch to go unclaimed—or else maybe he is gay, since Saugatuck, a mile from here, is the gay Mecca of the Midwest. And anyway, even if he is heterosexual and available, just the day before this, conferring with my counselor, I decided that I was going to stop looking for a man to date; if one fell into my lap, I told my counselor, I would reconsider, but I felt content, for the time being, to live my life without actively searching.

I started going to this counselor eight months ago, after Richard told me that he didn't want to marry me after all. Richard had agreed to go to counseling with me if our relationship ever faltered, but when the time came, he said, "I agreed to go to marriage counseling, and we're not married," so I ended up going by myself. Getting mostly over Richard, reaching the point where I didn't feel that I either needed him or needed to replace him, was a victory and a relief. I've been looking forward to a stretch of time untroubled by the uncertainties of romance, especially now that I feel strong again. Yet I don't come across a man who might suit me very often, and as Hal and I continue to talk, I begin to see in him the potential for something more than information about swimming in cold water.

I judge him to be around my age, forty-five. He tells me he is living for the fall and winter in his parents' lakeshore vacation house, from which he will soon start commuting to Indiana to work as an ER doctor. In the meantime, he is scouting around for a research fellowship and working on a science-fiction novel and several scientific essays.

I ask him what the essays are about, and he tells me that the one he's just finished is about the bioengineering of humans. He grins combatively, lifting his chin. "I'm in favor of it," he says.

"That's different. Most people aren't."

"No, they're not," he agrees. "But it's the only way we're going to change people enough to stop them from destroying each other and the planet. I'm calling that essay, 'Who's Afraid of a Brave New World?' In it, I argue that technology has outpaced our moral capacities and that the way to correct this is to bioengineer humans to make us more empathetic."

"That sounds like it might be a good idea," I say. "Do you have children?"

He lets out a sad laugh. "No, I'm a misanthrope. I don't want children. The world is overpopulated." He looks at me intently. "I was with a woman I loved very much—we're still very close—but I didn't marry her because she wants children and I don't."

"That's a significant difference," I say. "It's not as if you can compromise—have half a child instead."

He laughs and nods emphatically, seeming glad that I understand. I tell him that I'm divorced and that my daughter Marly is twenty-two and going to college to become a veterinary technician. I also tell him that I make my living as a bus driver and that I'm a writer.

We talk some more, with Hal doing most of the talking: about his former medical practice in Texas, about snorkeling in Lake Michigan and in the Caribbean, about the planets and the stars, which are beginning to show in the sky—by this time, night has fallen. "I better let you go," he says, his animated face barely visible in the dark. "Sorry for talking your ear off."

I tell him that I've had fun talking with him, and he says he hopes he runs into me again.

"Well, rather than relying on chance," I say, "why don't you give me your phone number?"

Hal laughs. "I don't know it yet, by heart. But it's in the phone book, under my dad's name, which is the same as mine: Hal McCord."

Later that night, sipping tea and eating pie with my women friends, one of them says, "You met *another* man on the beach?"

"Well, the beach is practically the only place I go, in public," I answer. "I don't go to bars, but I walk by the lake or the river almost every day."

⌒

I CALL HAL the following Tuesday, and he offers to loan me his wet suit and to show me how to snorkel. But whenever it's warm enough for snorkeling in the coming weeks, either I'm at work or Hal is off playing golf. Instead, we go for walks, I read his essay and he reads my stories; we talk about literature and argue about politics and he lectures me on science.

Some evenings we eat dinner together, when Hal isn't worrying that he might be coming down with the flu or some other virus to which he's possibly been exposed. If he's going to get sick, he says, he wants his stomach to be empty. At times he won't eat at all, and other times he finally starts in on his dinner as I am finishing mine. "You're a real worrier, aren't you?" I say one night, watching him pick up his fork and then set it down over and over without the tines ever reaching his plate.

"It's called neurotic," he answers.

One night Marly drives down from Grand Rapids to have dinner with us. Hal seems even more animated than usual— even though he wants no children of his own, it's clear that he wants my daughter to like him.

After I serve up the stir-fry, Hal lets his plate rest on the table in front of him without touching it while Marly and I eat. The conversation turns to the ethical differences between health care for humans and health care for animals, and Marly says, "I think we should consider putting down vicious people, like we do vicious dogs. Attack once, and that's it, you get the needle." Hal throws back his head and laughs up at the ceiling.

When Marly and I are halfway through our food and Hal still hasn't taken one bite, he asks me if I mind if he zaps his plate of stir-fry in the microwave. "No, go ahead," I say. He's already told me that he "autoclaves" his plate at family dinners. When I asked him what his big family—he has six siblings— thought of his doing that, Hal said, "Oh," and stopped, waving his hand, blushing. Finally he murmured, "They're used to me."

Now as Hal rises from the table and walks to the microwave, Marly keeps her eyes lowered. I've already warned her that Hal is weird about food. I wish I had put on some music for dinner; instead we sit listening to the microwave hum. When it dings, Hal retrieves his plate and sits down and asks Marly what she thinks of the ethics of bioengineering tomatoes to include the cells of fish.

"Well, it depends," Marly says. "Do they ask the fish first? And what about the tomatoes?" And Hal throws back his head and laughs again. Then he picks up his fork and begins, tentatively, to eat.

After he leaves, I ask Marly what she thinks of him. "He's okay," she says.

"What do you mean? Don't you like him?"

"I like him okay," Marly says.

"That's all you're going to tell me?"

"Okay, fine, Mom. I know I've called some of your other boyfriends nutty, but this one takes the cake. But at least it's a harmless sort of nuttiness. He seems like a decent guy."

⌣

ON CLEAR NIGHTS that autumn, Hal shows me Saturn with its band of rings through his telescope, and he points out Sirius and the Pleiades with his hand and his naked eye. We hold hands, and we run our hands over each other's shoulders and backs. One evening, lying down on Hal's parents' couch, we take off our sweaters and shirts, then press our half-naked bodies together and stroke each other and kiss. But Hal holds back from kissing me fully—it feels as if our tongues are playing hide-and-seek, with mine doing all the seeking. Finally I pull back from him and ask, "Don't you like to kiss?"

Hal smiles sheepishly. "I only really like to kiss when I'm having sex."

"So, it's all or nothing with you?" I ask. "I've heard of men like that."

"No, there's some middle ground—this isn't nothing, is it?"

"No, it's nice."

We decide to hold off on having sex because he might be leaving as early as January for a research fellowship in another state, and we don't want to get deeply involved and then have to part. "And you're still vulnerable, Annie," Hal says, "because of Richard." He smiles at me nervously, his chin lifted, his head nodding. "And," he admits a little later, his half-naked body stretched along the length of mine, "I'm kind of shy—inhibited, I guess. I either need to have sex with a woman before I get to know her too well, or else, after I know her very well."

"So, we've missed our window of opportunity?" I ask.

"Our first window," Hal says, laughing, hiding his face in my neck.

Skin against skin is so nice, I think, that I can wait indefinitely for sex.

⌣

ONE NIGHT WE GO to a contra dance with a string band and a caller. The township hall where the dance is held is warm and packed with people. As soon as we step inside, Hal turns to me and says, his eyebrows raised in alarm that is only partly a joke, "This place is one giant Petri dish." I give him a look that means *don't start*, and take his hand and line up with the other dancers.

The caller walks us through the first dance without music, and then the band strikes up an Irish reel. I steer Hal through the steps—allemande left, lady's chain, right-hand star, balance-and-swing—and he holds me and releases me, pulls me close and swings me, and my long red dress flies out around us in a circle. "I really like this," Hal says, as we promenade down the hall.

It's the kind of dancing where everyone trades partners several times in a single dance, and one woman who is temporarily paired with Hal exclaims, "Your hands are so soft! What do you do for a living?"

He's unemployed, I say in my head as I size her up: her hair is long and dyed black, and she is dressed more fetchingly than I am, but I don't think she actually looks any better than me.

"I'm a doctor," Hal says quietly, looking down at his feet.

"Oh!" the woman breathes out, and then she spends the rest of the dance trying to flirt with him. Hal reacts shyly, perhaps partly due to my sharp gaze.

But I have to admit that I also find Hal's being a doctor attractive. Doctors are smart and the good ones help people and, once they've paid off their school loans, they don't have to worry about money. Plus, my father was a doctor, a psychiatrist, now retired. And I'm impressed that, at the same time that Hal was earning his medical degree, he also earned a PhD in biology, commuting between Houston and Galveston to attend the two full-time, rigorous programs. He is the smartest man I've ever dated, with a photographic memory and a mind like a calculator. But of course there are some holes in his knowledge, one of which becomes evident during the evening's last dance.

The last dance is a waltz. Hal and I mostly stand on the floor and sway. Someone has flipped off all of the lights except for those that shine on the stage, leaving the dancers in near darkness. I like how Hal's body bumps and presses against mine, out of sync with the music; I like talking with him quietly in the dimness, our faces close: "Annie, tell me what I'm supposed to be doing."

"I hardly know how to do this myself."

"I'm screwing it up all up," Hal says, yanking my arm a little higher.

"We're both screwing it all up," I say, trying not to stumble over his feet.

"No, you know how to do this, and I don't."

"I don't, really."

Hal tries to steer me, or seems to. I don't follow, and our feet shuffle and our legs bobble at odd angles. "All I know," Hal says, "is you count to four."

"No, it's three."

"Are you sure? I think it's four."

"It's three," I say. "I'm sure it's three."

⌒

DURING THE EVENINGS that we spend at Hal's house, we are often interrupted by phone calls. Hal has a dozen friends across the country that he keeps in contact with by phone, three-quarters of them women and most of them married, and it is his women friends, especially the married ones, who phone most often. Sometimes when I'm at Hal's house, three or four call in one evening. Hal will say, "I can't talk now—Annie's here." It's a relief to me as well as a pleasure that Hal has told these other women of my presence in his life. But the pleasure pales when the women keep on talking.

"Why doesn't she talk with her husband?" I ask one night of Irinia, with whom Hal finished his residency. "Instead of always calling you with her complaints?"

"Her husband doesn't like to talk that much."

"Well, maybe she should give him another chance."

Hal begins to refrain from answering the phone when I'm at his house, but the alternative is not much better—instead, we stop talking or petting, as in a game of freeze, straining to hear who it is and what they are saying as they're being recorded. One night the same woman calls twice and leaves messages. I prick up my ears to hear her voice, but it's too soft to make out her words. I recognize this caller as Ling, Hal's former girlfriend with whom he still talks every couple of days. My consolation about this frequency of calls is that Ling is married and lives in North Carolina, that Hal calls me at least as often as he does her, and that we are seeing each other several times a week, but he hasn't seen Ling in over a year. Still, his attachment to Ling worries me. This is the woman he told me about when I first met him, whom he didn't marry because she wants children and Hal doesn't. Four years ago she married a man named Leonard instead, but they haven't yet tried to have children. Ling is busy with her career, doing scientific research for a large corporation, and since she is more than a decade younger than Hal and me—only twenty-nine—she still has time on her biological clock.

Thirty minutes after Ling leaves her second message, the phone rings again. Whoever it is listens to the answering machine's message and then hangs up. I feel Hal's whole body slump at the click. I've noticed that when Ling calls, Hal says, "I can't talk right now, I have a visitor," but when anyone else calls, he says, "I can't talk, Annie's here." Later that night I ask Hal if he thinks his feelings for Ling are holding him back from loving me, and he says yes.

The next morning he calls and asks me how I am doing. I answer, "I'm having second thoughts about spending so much time with you." Hal asks when we can talk about this in person. I tell him I'm planning to take a walk before work, and we decide to meet at his house.

Hal's parents have been up to Saugatuck for the weekend, and, to keep Hal company, they've left behind their dog, a golden retriever named Luna. Hal meets me at the door and then clips Luna to her leash, and we walk down the private lane from the house and across Lakeshore Drive and down the stairs to the beach. As soon as Hal unclips the chain, Luna sprints ahead of us, running into the waves and then rolling on the sand. Usually on our walks Hal shouts at her, "Luna, get up!" and Luna leaps to her feet. A few minutes later, she'll be down and rolling again, and Hal will again shout, "Luna, get up!" After a couple more repetitions of this, Hal will call Luna over to him and reprimand her in full sentences as she grovels at his feet: "Why do you behave so stupidly? I've told you a million times that I don't want you rolling in decaying fish and other debris. If you don't start listening to me, I'm going to leave you at home." Hal often calls Luna a dumb dog, a victim of inbreeding, an evolutionary mistake. But today, rather than criticizing Luna or trying to control her, Hal leaves her to her own devices.

It starts to snow, heavily, as we walk along the shore. Usually we walk with my hand in Hal's and both our hands slipped into his coat pocket, but now we move independently, our arms dangling at our sides. "It doesn't feel right to be spending so much time with you when you're so attached to someone else," I say.

"Ling will always be part of my life," Hal answers.

"What does her husband think about you talking with her on the phone almost every day?"

"I don't know."

"It can't be good for their marriage," I say. "For him or for her. Or for you."

"I know, I've thought of that."

"Then why don't you stop?"

"I don't know. I guess I'm just a loyal person."

"Well, you're far more loyal to her than she is to you. She's married, Hal. She's living with her husband, seeing him every day, spending every evening with him, having sex with him."

"I know all that."

"Do you ever think about the fact of her having sex with her husband?"

"Not a lot, but yes."

"Why not a lot? She's probably having sex with him a lot."

"You're too fixated on sex," Hal says.

"No I'm not. I just want you to look at it squarely."

"She'll always be a part of my life," Hal says. "I can't forget her."

"It's hard to forget someone if you're talking with her constantly," I say. "And there's a difference between remembering someone and not letting her go."

Glancing up at the falling snow, I notice that our footsteps have veered from the water's edge; while slanting his face away from my verbal barrage, Hal's footsteps have veered away from me, too, and, without realizing it, my feet and body have followed his. I stop walking, and Hal looks up and sees where we are, and we turn back to a path parallel to the shoreline.

"Once she has children," Hal says, "I know things will change. Once she has a child, that will be the final nail in the coffin of our relationship."

"A relationship that's been over with for six years."

"I know it sounds strange, Annie. All my friends and family think so, too. I don't blame you for feeling like you do. If I were you, I'd feel how you're feeling now, and if you don't want to see me anymore, I'll understand. But I still want to see you. I like you a lot."

"You like me, but you don't love me," I say.

"It takes me a long time to fall in love."

We walk a few steps without speaking. "How long did it take you to fall in love with Ling?" I ask.

Hal squints into the distance. "About nine months."

I calculate how long Hal and I have known each other—though it seems like more, it has been only six weeks—and I wonder if Hal might fall in love with me in the future. I have started to fall in love with him, but I distrust the feeling. There are several men I've loved in the past whom I no longer love at all and about whom I now wonder, *What was I thinking?* And I also distrust feelings of love because of what happened with Richard.

My counselor has said that relationships are difficult and complicated and that Richard was not ready for one, and he has suggested that I go slowly and hold off on having sex with Hal, since sex—no matter what people think they can handle, my counselor says—is a bigger step than people make it out to be. My counselor has called Hal "a mystery, a big question mark," but he has surprised me by seeming to approve of him more than of Richard. But considering this new development, my counselor might change his opinion. I pull back my coat sleeve and look at the face of my watch. Snow swirls outside it, like a snow globe in reverse. I have to be at work in thirty minutes. "We should head back," I say, and we turn around.

The snow is now slanting at us, hitting our faces. It is thick and wet and stinging. Hal and I walk with our heads down, not saying much. As we near the stairs leading up from the beach, the storm suddenly abates, leaving behind only a few stray, floating flakes. Hal looks up and scans the rough lake, then glances worriedly at my face. "You're very important to me, Annie," he says. "I'd hate to stop seeing you. But I'll leave it up to you." He takes my hand and grips it tight, and we start up the wooden walkway with Luna thumping up behind us.

At the top of stairs Hal says, "Ling is going back to China soon, for a month. She's going to talk to her parents about having a child."

"Why? Does she need their permission?"

"Oh, no. Ling doesn't let anyone tell her what to do. She just wants to talk with them about it."

Hal bends to clip Luna to her leash, and I look behind us, out over the lake. I always like to face the lake one last time before leaving it, to try to impress it on my memory, to draw in what I can of its magnificence and power. I watch the waves roll and crash, sweep my gaze one more time across the horizon, then turn back to Hal and say, "A man I was in love with once told me, after it was clear that we wouldn't be together in the future, 'Love doesn't die, it just goes to live in a quieter place.' That's how I feel about him now, and also about another man who was important to me. I still love them in some way, but they're in the past. I couldn't have a day-to-day life if they were still in it. There's not enough room for everyone."

"Once she has a child," Hal says, "I know things will change."

⌒

DURING A COUNSELING session, as I talk about Hal's recent behavior in a restaurant, Greg listens with an amused look that grows more and more amused until finally he is grinning. The same is true of me: as I tell Greg this story, and at other times as well—when I tell Greg or my family or my friends about things Hal has said or done—my lips begin to curve upward and spread outward and soon I feel my teeth showing. "Why do you think this is funny?" I say to Greg. "Why do I think this is funny?" I've been talking about Hal refusing to eat in a restaurant because he noticed a waiter coughing into a napkin.

"Well, it's funny now that it's over," Greg says. "When you were in the midst of it, I'm sure you felt somewhat different."

"Yes, it was annoying," I say, still smiling. "We ended up getting back in the car and driving to another restaurant. And it was a used napkin, too. It's not as if the waiter was going to refold it and put it back on our table."

Both of us laugh again. Greg pushes his feet against the floor so that his chair gives a bounce, like a nod. Then he says,

"Hal is a nice guy, in many ways. There's a lot that's appealing about him. But you've said that you would like a relationship that will last the rest of your life. You *do* know what the chances are of him settling down with one person?"

"What?" I say. "What are they?" I know the chances aren't good, but I want to hear just how bad they are.

Greg waits for me to look at him. I do. He is alert, leaning toward me, no longer smiling. His eyes loom very large and somber. Holding my gaze with his own, he lifts his right hand and forms a circle with his thumb and finger, and then he holds his hand motionless like that, in a zero formation, as if to burn the shape into my consciousness. Finally, he speaks. "About that," he says.

About that, I think. *Almost* nothing. Then that means, although it's very slight, there is still *some* hope.

⌣

FOR CHRISTMAS, I give Hal *Best American Science and Nature Writing* and another book, and he gives me my choice of magazine subscription and a large photo of a black lake in the Yukon with the northern lights coloring the sky. Lying on my couch with Hal after we've exchanged gifts, I say, "I thought not having sex would help us keep more emotional distance, but I'm feeling so close to you anyway."

Hal tightens his grip on me and confesses, "I'm feeling really close to you, too."

"It feels like I've known you for more than three months," I say.

"It feels like a lot more than that," Hal agrees. He presses his face into my neck, and I wonder if he is trying to get even closer to me, or if he is hiding from what he's just said.

⌒

I AM SCHEDULED to dispatch for the bus company's late New Year's Eve shift, but on the day before it, I swap my shift for an earlier one, and by the time I know that I have the night free, Hal has made his own plans: he is going in to his parents' house in Chicago to take care of Luna (his parents are spending New Year's Eve in Wisconsin and don't want to leave the dog in a kennel) and Hal's friend Julie is driving down from Madison to spend New Year's with him. I've met Julie, and even though I'm sure that she is not a sexual threat, I'm somewhat jealous that Hal will be spending New Year's Eve with her instead of with me. I remind myself that I was indecisive about freeing up the night so that I could spend it with Hal—at one point, he even suggested that he sleep over at my house—and I reconcile myself to spending my suddenly free evening with a few of my book club friends.

Five days after New Year's Eve, while I am at work, Hal leaves a message on my answering machine that he is back from Chicago, and he invites me out to dinner. He arrives at my house around seven, and we get in his car and drive to The Blue Moon, a new restaurant whose food and décor are both casual and elegant. But we haven't made reservations, and the next opening is at nine thirty and it's only quarter to eight, so we get back in the car and continue down the road to the Blue Star Diner.

I've had a bad feeling all day about seeing Hal this evening, and sitting across the booth from him, ordering from the laminated menus in the diner's bright light and then waiting for our food, our conversation flags and my fears increase. Hal seemed to prolong his stay in Chicago unnecessarily, and he sounded vague and evasive the few times he phoned me, and now that he is finally back in town and alone with me, he doesn't seem that glad to see me. Throughout dinner, I feel as distant and disengaged as he seems to be. Still, after we've eaten, hoping to turn the evening around, I say, "Do you want to go over to my house for a while?"

"No, Annie," he says, "I'm really tired. And I have to get up early tomorrow and drive to Kalamazoo to help Irinia finish up that project."

"I thought you were finished with that project," I say. He's been helping Irinia with the same project, mostly over the phone, since I met him.

"All the research is done—we just need to write it up."

"So why do you have to get up early to do that?"

"Because it's going to take all day." He looks down at his half-finished gyros. "So—I want to get a good night's sleep, go right home after I drop you off." He waits a couple of seconds. "Is that okay with you?"

"Not really," I say.

He sighs and mutters, "I didn't think it would be."

"You've been gone for five days," I say. I look at my watch. "And it's not even nine o'clock."

Hal glances around the diner. The only people besides us in the small, brightly lit room are Marcos, the owner, and Lizzy, the lone waitress. "Let's get going," Hal says.

We get into Hal's car, and as we drive out the winding river road to my house, we argue some more. Suddenly Hal says, "I don't see why we had to get close so fast!"

I think of how, after three months, we still haven't gotten past making out while naked from the waist up. "We're not that close," I say dryly.

"I'm talking about emotionally, Annie!" Hal says, striking the steering wheel with his hand.

I tilt my head away to hide my smile, amused by his intensity and pleased that he feels close to me.

At my house, I make tea and cut two pieces of carrot cake, and we carry the steaming mugs and plates of cake to the couch and set them on the windowsill behind us. Hal sits on the couch with his feet on the floor looking resigned yet tense, while I lounge next to him in my normal fashion, with my legs and feet crossed yoga-style. I take Hal's hand and hold it. His hand in mine feels limp, unresponsive. "I think you don't find me attractive enough," I say.

"You're attractive," he says, as if he doubts his own words. "Sometimes I think you're very attractive."

I hold his limp hand thinking of what a pallid word "attractive" is. And "sometimes" isn't such a hot word, either.

"You have a cute way about you," Hal says, giving my hand a light squeeze.

"Do you think being in love with Ling is still getting in your way?" I ask.

"Yes," he says. Then he tells me that Ling has left for China. But instead of going to talk with her parents about having a child, Hal says, she is going to talk with them about getting divorced. "She and Leonard are not getting along too well," Hal says with a happy note in his voice. "She says she feels closer to me than she does to him."

I draw back all at once, slipping my hand from Hal's and setting my feet on the floor and shifting my body away. Sitting up straight with my feet and hands pulled in close to me, I notice that my body is self-contained and aligned with itself.

I could do that again, I think—align myself with myself, live my own, separate life.

"That's the opposite direction of where she was heading before," I say to Hal. "You said that having a child would be the final nail in the coffin, and then you could move on."

"I know."

"So how do you feel now?"

"That I can't go ahead in another relationship until I get the green light from Ling."

I stand up in a rush. Behind me, on the windowsill, are our two plates of cake. I pick up my plate and snatch up the fork. I could hit him in the face with the cake, grind the cream-cheese frosting into his mouth and nose like a slighted bride. Or I could stab him with the fork. Not in the eye or neck or anywhere vital—although it would serve him right if I gave a good stab to his balls. Hal has stood up, too, with a startled look in his eyes, and has shuffled a few feet backward from me.

"Let me get this straight," I say, pointing my fork as if it were my index finger. "You can't live your life and love anyone else without permission from your ex-girlfriend who is married."

"I know that sounds crazy," Hal says.

"It is crazy. I don't see how you can be happy like that."

"I don't want to be happy."

I look into his eyes. They are sorrowful and resigned now rather than startled. He looks as if he wants or at least expects to be stabbed. "You don't want to be happy?"

"No," he says.

"Why not?"

"It's just not something that I care to be."

It occurs to me that he is being un-American, but I don't want to point this out and turn our confrontation into a joke. Instead I think about what he might mean and about what my feelings are in relation to my own happiness. As I contemplate this, my hand holding the fork sinks into the edge of my slice of cake, releasing the fragrance of cream cheese and walnuts and spice. I lift a small bite into my mouth, press hard, and chew and swallow. "Well, I guess happiness is not really my goal, either," I say. "I think being satisfied is a better way of describing what I want—I want to be satisfied with my life."

"Yes, that's what I want, too."

I set the fork back down onto my plate, and Hal grabs up my free hand and holds it tight; I wonder if his intent is to disarm me, physically and emotionally.

"So, what do you want to do?" I ask. "What do you want our relationship to be?"

"I want to keep seeing you. I want it to continue on, be what it is." He is gazing down at the floor and looking sheepish, gripping my hand even harder. I think of upending the cake on the top of his head, melding the frosting with his thinning hair. I also think of how I can't say to him, "You've just been using me for sex!" Accusing him of using me for friendship, or even for cuddling and light petting, just doesn't have the same ring.

⁓

THROUGHOUT THE FOLLOWING day, Hal calls and leaves a series of lengthy but vague messages. It's Sunday, and I'm at home, but I don't answer the phone. I spend several hours writing in my journal, and I also clean out a closet and go for a long walk.

The next morning I call Hal and announce, "I've decided to stop seeing you."

"Okay, Annie," Hal says quietly.

"Do you want to talk about it in person, or over the phone?"

There is a longish pause. Then he says, "In person."

By the time I get off work and drive over to Hal's house, all that's left of the sunset is a narrow stripe of salmon pink at the horizon. As we start off toward the lake, Hal wraps his arm around my shoulder and leans his head over me sideways so that his head is above mine. I shrink a little and consider jabbing him with my elbow. He tightens his arm, pulling me close against his side, and we walk like that, with me held in his encircling, sideways, and, I have to admit, comfortable embrace.

I come right out with it. "The reason I don't want to see you anymore is because of this new thing you told me about Ling—that she's thinking about getting a divorce now and feels closer to you than to her husband. The last time we talked about this, you said that her having a child would end things for you. Well, now it's taken a huge step in the opposite direction."

I pause, waiting for him to respond, but he just keeps walking, holding me tightly.

"And also your saying that you can't move ahead in another relationship until you get the green light from Ling. She just has too much control over your life. You're not available. I'm spending way too much time with you, considering that you're not available."

"You're an intelligent woman, Annie," Hal says. "You're being very reasonable." There is a humorous, wry note in his voice, as if intelligence and reason have nothing to do with this.

"Well, that's how I'm trying to be. I'm just trying to make a good decision." I had vowed not to get involved again with a man who was ambivalent or unavailable, but it seems that I've fallen right back into my same old pattern. That needs to change, and since Hal isn't going to give up on Ling, I have to give up on Hal.

Hal continues to hold me with his arm wrapped around me in a sideways crush, and my anger softens to sadness. We walk quietly to the end of the lane and look out at the intensely deep pink, narrowing strip of sky. "Is this what you wanted to show me?" Hal says.

"Yes, though it's disappearing."

"It's still beautiful, though."

We stroll up and down Lakeshore Drive, gazing at the rapidly fading pink streak and the blue-black sky taking its place, then turn back on the lane toward his house.

"Sometimes I wonder if you're just using Ling as an excuse to not get very involved with anyone else," I say. "That way, you can have this feeling of love without having it be completely real, and you can still have your own life to yourself. You can have lots of friends, and this one, long-lost love, but still have the freedom to go wherever you want and hole up like a hermit and not deal with any one person too intimately."

"Well, I know that people have unconscious motives," Hal says. "I'm not sure that those are what mine are, but you might be right."

We walk back to the house and let out Luna, who is ecstatic that we've decided not to leave her behind after all. With Luna running ahead of us, Hal and I walk down the lane again, this time away from the lake, toward the woods. A thin layer of snow covers the ground, more than at my house, where the surface is only dusted.

I'm not sure what to say. It occurs to me that I haven't

broken up with anyone since high school—all my boyfriends since then, and even my husband, broke up with me. Though in the case of my husband, it was more complicated, since by the time he asked me to leave, my love for him was long gone. It had died with the death of our first baby girl, and even the birth of our second, healthy girl hadn't revived it.

Hal and I walk in circles and loops through the woods in the light snow. "This is hard," he says. "I don't like to see you sad. And it makes me sad, too. I really care for you. I care for you a lot."

"Well, maybe we can see each other sometimes," I say. I don't know what to suggest—once every three weeks, once every two weeks? A break of a few weeks, then see what feels right? "I don't know how often," I say.

"I'll honor whatever you want to do, Annie."

We step from the snow-lit darkness of the leafless hardwoods into the deeper darkness of evergreens, and the snow deepens to blue under our feet. We are walking holding hands in our usual way—my hand in his and both our hands tucked into his coat pocket, since he never remembers to wear gloves. Although the air has grown dark, the snow at our feet is bright enough for us to see by.

"Marly is going to talk to her doctor tomorrow about switching to a different anxiety medication," I say.

"Why?"

"Because she doesn't like the side effects of the one she's on now. She tried stopping it altogether last week, but she got so panicky, she couldn't even leave the house. Now she's back on it, and she's calm again, but she wants to try something else."

"Can I call you tomorrow night and talk with you about it? After you find out what her doctor says?" Hal asks.

"Okay," I say.

We chat some more, and then we are silent. We are making our way back toward the house when Hal suddenly says, "There's a chance that I can put Ling behind me and be committed to you."

I stiffen but keep walking.

"If I'd met you before Ling," Hal says, "I'd be in love with you."

It's a nice thought, but I don't like its effect—my resolve to leave Hal is now turning around. As he must have suspected it would. As I feel hope seeping back from wherever it disappeared to, I remind myself that neither of Hal's statements at all changes where things currently stand.

"I want to take you back by a different way," Hal says. "Around by the back of the house. Is that all right?"

I say okay, and he veers off the path holding my hand, out of his pocket now. We walk through brush and woods. Soon, up ahead, we see the back of his house. I've never seen it from the backside before, and approaching it at night from this angle feels as if we are doing something slightly illegal, or spying, at the very least, though no one is home for us to spy on or frighten.

"What about going to the contra dances?" Hal says. "Does this mean that going to the dances is out?" We've gone to two more dances since the first one.

"I don't know," I say. This whole breakup is falling apart.

"Are you sorry you met me?" Hal asks. We are still making our way, like criminals, through the twigs and undergrowth behind Hal's parents' house.

"No," I say, uncertainly.

"Well, I'm not sorry I met you." He sounds angry and hurt.

I hold a branch back from my face. More twigs snap under our feet.

"What have you done with your other old boyfriends?" Hal demands.

I laugh. "Stabbed them to death with a fork. Buried them out in the backyard."

We walk up to the rear of the house. I wonder if Hal has led me this way hoping that I'll go in. But I don't choose the back stairs and neither does Hal—we slowly circle around to the side door, a few steps beyond which my car is parked, and hug good-bye. I'm beginning to cry.

"I do think you're beautiful, Annie," Hal says. "Sometimes I think you're extraordinarily beautiful." This is quite a bit different from having a cute way about me, and he is again prefacing his compliment with "sometimes," but I'm not going to argue with him about that now. I turn my head sideways so that he can't see me crying.

"I care for you very much, Annie," Hal says.

"Not enough," I say. "You still need permission to love me."

"I think you underestimate how much I care about you."

"It's still not enough," I say.

"I don't want to stop seeing you."

"I don't know what else to do," I say. His face looks red and shiny and wet, as if he's been crying, although I haven't noticed any tears leaving his eyes.

"I'll miss seeing your smiling face," Hal says.

"It's not smiling much lately," I say, realizing as I say it that I am smiling now, albeit sadly.

"I'll miss you scolding me for being politically conservative."

I smile some more.

"So, can I call you tomorrow and see how Marly's appointment went?" he asks.

"Yeah."

"Around nine o'clock?"

"Yeah."

We start walking toward my car.

"I'm going to keep calling you until you tell me I can't anymore," Hal says.

"Okay."

"I'm going to show up at book club," he says.

"You never came even when you were invited."

"I'm going to start lurking around the bus station."

I smile again.

At my car, we embrace. I don't want to let him go. I pull back from him and look at him. His face looks odd—sad and mysterious and somewhat blank, his smile ghostlike. We embrace once more, and I get into my car. As I am reversing out of the driveway, I remember with a stab that I haven't said good-bye to Luna. But then I realize that I'll probably be back.

⌒

HAL CALLS ME the next evening and asks how Marly's appointment went.

"Really well," I say. "Her doctor is phasing her off her old med and introducing the new one at the same time. So the switch should go smoothly. And he thinks the new medication will work better."

"That's good news," Hal says. Then he tells me that he had a bad day. I ask him why, and he says, "I'm sad, Annie. I'm sad for you and for me. I missed you today."

I realize that I haven't missed Hal because I was relieved

I would see him again; I was glad that our breakup wasn't complete—maybe not even a breakup at all. I also realize now that I haven't shared this news with Hal.

"What if we see each other once a week?" I say. "And talk on the phone a couple of times?"

"That sounds good, Annie," Hal answers. "That would be great."

⌒

OVER THE NEXT few days we talk on the phone briefly twice, and on the fifth day after our breakup we go for a walk. When we return, we lie down on Hal's couch with our bodies entangled. I run my fingers through Hal's hair, rubbing his scalp. "I really love it when you do that," he says. The phone rings, and he buries his head in my chest. I try not to listen to who it is. When whatever woman it is has finished leaving her message, we relax again. We lie down together for a long time, keeping our clothes on, talking inconsequentially.

Two nights later, we go out to dinner at The Blue Moon, then come back to my house. Soon we are lying together on my couch listening to CDs, including several I got for Christmas, and lazily talking while we stroke each other through our sweaters.

Our bodies begin to heat up. Hal helps me remove my sweater and I do the same for him. Then I begin unbuttoning his shirt. "Can I take this off?" I ask.

"Ohh," Hal groans, "I've gotten fat from eating Christmas fudge. I don't want you to see my belly."

"I can turn the lights off," I say. "Then you'll be invisible."

Hal laughs. "Okay."

I sit up and turn off the lamp, casting the room in total

darkness. Someone on my CD player is singing a fast song with mumbled lyrics. I peel off Hal's shirt, entangling his head and his wrists because I haven't opened enough of the buttons. We laugh and struggle in the darkness until I have freed him, and then he helps me pull off my shirt, and we press our half-bare bodies together.

The song with mumbled lyrics ends, and the random-select whirrs and a clear, twangy voice rings out:

Love is strange,
Getting stranger

My face breaks into a smile, but I don't say anything. Hal can't see me in the dark and I can't see him.

Growing stronger,
That's the danger—
We've got a strange kind of love.

Hal clutches me tighter. Then his body begins to spasm with silent laughter, and then we both start laughing out loud.

⌣

THE NEXT FEW TIMES Hal and I see each other, before or after we have dinner, instead of lying down on the couch, we go to bed. We take off most and sometimes all of our clothes, yet we both are still holding back. I've begun to feel that we can't keep to this pattern much longer: going up to the edge without going over. Hal has told me three or four times since our supposed breakup that he loves me, but he always follows it up with the warning, "but I'm leaving soon, Annie." It is February, and he has to be out of his parents' house by the end of May, when his many siblings will start using the house for vacations with their families.

Throughout the month of March, Hal travels to interviews—one in Utah, another in California, and a third in West Virginia. One night during dinner at his house, he tells me that he's been offered a fellowship in West Virginia.

"So you came across better than you thought," I say, looking up from the piece of potato I've just cut. "Good for you. Do you think you'll take it?"

"I don't know. I'd like to do the other interviews first."

"That makes sense." Hal has interviews lined up at Dartmouth and NYU.

"And I got another interview. In North Carolina. In Wake Forest." Hal holds very still, gripping his knife, which is embedded in his steak, as if bracing for a blow.

"Oh," I say. I sit as still as Hal. Wake Forest is where Ling lives. I don't think Hal will get involved with her again—he didn't the last time he visited her and her husband, over a year ago. But Ling has been considering divorce in the time since, so things might play out differently now.

Hal fidgets with his fork, and then he sets it down. "Wake Forest has a very good program. And it's in a high-tech medical corridor. But West Virginia has a very good program, too. And I was their top choice out of four hundred applicants."

"Well, congratulations," I say. "Good for you."

After we finish dinner, we go for a walk. We walk especially far that evening, and by the time we get back, it's late. We lie down together and stroke each other a little but not much. We keep our clothes on. The following night, I run my fingers through Hal's hair, sitting beside him on the couch, but he only smiles sadly and otherwise doesn't respond. As I'm leaving his house, he says that he plans to spend the next day in Kalamazoo with Irinia learning something new about how to read EKGs.

A thread of jealousy twines through me. I try to ignore it. "Well, do you want to get together in the evening, then, when you get back?" I ask. "I have tomorrow night free, but on Wednesday, I have my quilting group." I've skipped going to quilting before to spend the evening with Hal, but I don't want to skip it now—I know I need to keep seeing the people in my life who will remain in it after Hal is gone.

"I'm not sure what time I'm getting back tomorrow," Hal says. "Why don't we just go for a walk on Wednesday?"

"Because I'll only have about an hour between work and quilting on Wednesday," I say. "Tomorrow, we'd have more time."

"Well, tomorrow isn't going to work for me," Hal says. "Why don't we just go for a short walk on Wednesday, and then we can go out for dinner or something on Friday?"

The next morning, I stride around my house, packing a lunch for work and laying out clothes while fuming to myself. I wish I could talk with my counselor. I haven't gone to see him since January, because he got mixed up about when my insurance's calendar year starts and ends, and we didn't space my twenty allotted appointments accordingly, and I used them all up. I could still come talk to him in February and March, Greg told me, but I'd have to pay the full price, which is nine-ty-eight dollars an hour.

HAL CALLS ME the following night after he's returned from Irinia's to say that he can't walk with me on Wednesday after all, because he's driving to Chicago to buy a suit.

"You're driving all the way to Chicago to buy a suit?" I say. "Why don't you get one in Grand Rapids?"

"Because my mom knows a good place in Chicago."

"There are good places in Grand Rapids," I say. "And why do you need a suit, anyway?"

"For my interviews," Hal says.

"Why don't you just wear the one you wore in Utah and West Virginia?"

"That wasn't a suit, it was just a sport jacket. My mom thinks it isn't good enough."

"It was good enough for Utah to still be considering you and for West Virginia to choose you over everyone else. And why do you need to run off to get the suit tomorrow? And cancel our plans?"

"Because I'm leaving to go out east on Saturday. Or else Sunday or Monday."

"Tomorrow is only Wednesday, and your next interview isn't until next Wednesday."

"I'm going to try to get one of them moved up, since I've added the one in Wake Forest. And I didn't think they were such big plans—we were only going for a walk. I thought our bigger plan was for Friday—going out to eat. I can be back from Chicago by Friday."

"I've hardly seen you lately, and now you're leaving again, driving all the way to Chicago just to buy a suit."

"Well, I might not buy one. I might get one from my uncle. My uncle who lives in Chicago."

"This just isn't working," I say quietly, as much to myself as to Hal. "This just isn't working for me. We're going to have to be just friends, Hal."

~

HAL CALLS ME the next morning to say that he isn't going in to Chicago to buy the suit and he is also canceling his trip east. "I accepted the job in West Virginia," he says. "It's a good offer, and I might not get a better one. They wanted me to decide quickly, and I figured it would be better to not make them wait."

"Well, congratulations," I say. "How do you feel about it?"

"I think it will be good. They've got an excellent program. It's not the best in the country, but it's really very prestigious, Annie."

"Well, good for you," I say.

"So, do you still want to go for a walk today?" Hal asks.

⌒

WE CONTINUE TO GO for walks and to eat dinner together, but we never resume our previous level of intimacy. We are like puppies from the same litter, snuggling together for comfort and warmth. A couple of times when we do become aroused, Hal pulls away from me. "Well, we really are just friends," I say, as much to myself as to Hal.

We continue to see each other about three times a week. Then it drops back to two or sometimes just one. Hal still calls, though less often. When my dad is diagnosed with Parkinson's and I'm concerned about that, and when I'm considering refinancing my house, Hal talks both issues through with me during several phone calls and offers extensive and helpful advice. In short, he is a good friend.

At times during the couple of months after we've scaled back to just friendship, I look at Hal and think that he is very handsome. Sometimes I think of all the things I like about him—his intelligence, his humor, his intensity, his passionate convictions, even the ones I don't agree with, and also, that he is kind and at base a good person, and I start thinking that maybe it can work—a lasting and romantic, sexual relationship with him. But then I remember the other things—that he's ambivalent about love and sex, that he hasn't given up on Ling, that he's never settled down with any one person or in any one place for very long.

I start seeing my counselor again early in April, and during our second appointment I ask him, "What's wrong with me? Why can't I figure relationships out?"

Greg answers: "I think, if I were in your place, I wouldn't have done any better with Richard. I think he would have fooled me, too. Not that he meant to."

"And what about Hal?"

Greg looks down at his knees, nodding his head. "He's very appealing, in many ways," he says. "But I think you could have figured that one out sooner."

"Why did it take me so long?" I ask.

Greg raises his eyebrows as if to say, *What do you think?* Even though we've had a two-month break, we've been doing this long enough that he sometimes uses signals rather than words to get me to answer my own questions.

"Because I didn't want to go through another breakup," I say. "And there are a lot of things I like about him, and I was enjoying his company. And I tend to hope even when there isn't much reason to."

"Hope's not about reason, is it," Greg says.

"But it seems that I should know more about men than I do by now."

"What do you think you should know?" Greg asks.

"How to get in a good relationship and stay in it."

"That's a lifelong pursuit," Greg says, "dependent partly on luck. You're a strong person and you have a good life as it is, but you would do well in a relationship. Just don't let your desire for a partner make you forget what you want for yourself."

"I still don't see how I'm going to find a partner."

Greg throws up his hands, smiling faintly. He's already told me many times that finding a good partner is difficult, especially in mid-life. "I can't help you with that," he says, "other than the usual advice of asking people to set you up, getting out more, keeping your eyes and your mind open. Maybe someday, if I get out of this business, I'll go into matchmaking, but for now that's not my department."

"Well, it doesn't seem like I've learned very much."

Greg hunkers down in his chair and eyes me kindly. "You're learning," he says. "Slowly, but that's how most learning works. It took you longer than it might have to determine that Hal makes a better friend than he does a mate, but you learned it, and you did it with reason and with certitude and without an emotional upheaval."

"But it took me six months!"

Greg lifts his eyebrows and his shoulders in a shrug. "It would have taken some people a couple of years," he says. "It would take others more than a lifetime."

⌒

ALL THROUGH APRIL and May, Hal and I talk about going snorkeling soon, now that the lake will be warming up again. But both the lake and the air temperatures remain unseasonably cold. Finally, late in May, despite the cold temperatures, we set a date for the afternoon.

A few hours before we are supposed to go, Hal calls me

and says that he'll still go if I want to, but we will probably freeze our butts off. "I'm not backing out," he says. "You keep telling me that I always cancel plans and change my mind, but that's not true."

"It is true," I insist, smiling into the receiver. "You always cancel and change."

"I do not, and I'm not canceling this plan—if you want to go, I'll go. I'm used to freezing water, but you're not, so I thought you might rather go for a walk." I think of the first time I saw Hal, walking with his bare feet in the cold water. It was on the day that I first met him, when he told me about looking at rocks and fish and lines etched into the lake bottom.

"We can put it off again," I say. "We can go for a walk instead."

I drive to Hal's house, and we take the stairs to the beach. He is wearing a windbreaker and slacks, and I have on jeans and a fleece jacket. Hal is leaving in three weeks or so, for a two-month job in Minnesota. Maybe he'll come back to his parents' vacation house in the fall, he says, or maybe he'll go to Alaska, or to some other place he hasn't yet determined, and work until March, when the fellowship in West Virginia begins.

"You'll know what you're doing when you do it," I tease. It no longer bothers me that his future plans are unsettled, since I no longer imagine that his future will include me.

"But when I move to West Virginia, I *am* going to buy thirty or forty acres and a small house," Hal says. "Kind of like your house—that's a good size. Three bedrooms would be right for me—one for my bedroom, one for my study, and one for guests."

"That does sound right for you," I agree.

Hal lifts his head suddenly and looks up the beach. "Luna!" he shouts. A hundred yards from us, Luna is rolling on the sand. "Darwin was wrong," Hal says. "That dog should have been bred out of existence." Then he takes off running up the beach after her.

I pick up a stick of driftwood and rinse it in the lake, watching the grit and sand clear from its surface. I hope that Hal will buy a house in West Virginia and that he will like it. I think of how I won't share it with him. Most likely, I won't even visit.

During a recent counseling session, Greg joked: "Well, at least you'll have a friend for life—he'll be calling you once a week for the rest of your life."

But Hal won't call that often—even if he wanted to, I wouldn't let him. Maybe I'll call him, once a year or so. If I do, when he picks up the phone, I'll ask if he's alone. I'll get off the phone quickly if someone is with him. And I'll wonder if it's someone like me—or rather, someone like who I was: a woman waiting for him to give her his full attention.

A hundred yards up the beach, Hal is leaning down to Luna and giving her a lecture. I can see his lips moving but cannot hear what he is saying, although I know him well enough by now to guess. I look out at the lake, past the second sandbar, where the waves are strong and breaking. A few weeks from now, I will be swimming out there, without a wet suit and by myself.

Hands

"REMEMBER MY FRIEND BRAD?" Marly asks as we are eating Sunday dinner in my kitchen. With her curved, dainty hand, she picks up a calzone.

"Remind me," I say.

"He was in my very first photo class at GRCC. He works at Literary Lights. He came to your reading there, three years ago."

"Oh, sure," I say. "Tall, thin, blond?"

Marly nods and bites into the steaming pastry and spicy pork.

"He seemed shy but really sweet," I say. "Didn't you date him for a while?"

Marly chews and swallows and fans her face. "Depends on what you call a date. At first, we were just friends. We went on a few photo expeditions together. We kissed a few times.

Then one night we made out, and he totally freaked—he said he had to go, and he jumped up and left my apartment. I tried calling him, about five different times, but he never answered my messages." She sips from her glass of milk. "I haven't seen him, or even talked to him, in almost three years. But now he called me, last week, and he wants to get together. He says he's not sure if he can be more than friends, and he asked me if that was all right."

"What did you say?"

"I told him friends was fine."

⌒

MIDWEEK MARLY CALLS and asks if she can bring Brad and her longtime pal Atom over for dinner on Sunday. "We'll be down that way shooting more abandoned houses."

"Sure, bring them along," I say.

"Oh, and Brad wants to show you his portfolio, if that's okay."

"That's fine," I say. "But why does he want me to see his work?"

"He thinks you're kind of cool. In your own incredibly uncool way, I mean. He's impressed that you're a published writer."

"The world needs more people like him," I say.

"Okay, then, we'll come over around five or six, whenever we're done. Atom found some more wrecked houses in Pullman that we want to explore."

"Trespassing in Pullman doesn't sound very safe, Marly." Pullman, where Atom lives with his dad, is an impoverished community a half hour southeast of my house—a stark, one-bar town surrounded by a rural scattering of mostly decrepit dwellings, more than a few of which have been abandoned. "I wish you'd take photos of nature or something," I say, "instead of poking around Pullman."

"Mom, you worry too much. I wouldn't shoot there alone. That's why the three of us are going together."

THAT SUNDAY, I mix up a double batch of tofu burgers, a recipe I've come up with that pleases even dedicated carnivores. As I snip basil from my garden and then straighten up the house, I wonder how Marly and Brad will manage as "just friends." It isn't a new concept for Marly. Atom has always been just her friend, ever since they were thirteen, and they are now twenty-three. Once I let slip my assumption that at some point Atom had been her lover, and Marly had hooted and said, "Sex with Atom? That would be like having sex with my brother, if I had a brother. Besides," she added, "a girl needs a boy friend who isn't a boyfriend."

Just after six o'clock, Marly, Atom, and Brad arrive in a swirl of dust—my unpaved road and driveway are parched from drought—and clomp up onto my front porch and open the door, bringing the scent of mint and sweat into my living room. Marly leads the way, laughing at something Atom has said. Atom follows next, looming high above my diminutive daughter, and when he looks up from stomping his dusty boots on the mat, I'm surprised by how handsome he is, his dark hair and pale skin and strong, even features uncluttered with his usual nine pieces of facial jewelry. "Atom, you look so nice without all that metal," I say. "I can see your face—and you have a really nice face."

Atom grins. "Oh, this is just temporary," he says. "I had to remove it for a job interview at Menard's this morning, and I haven't had a chance yet to reinsert."

After I've finished admiring Atom's metal-free face, Brad surfaces from removing his athletic shoes and says hi to me with the sweet, shy smile and observant eyes I remember from three years ago. He isn't as handsome as Atom—Brad's blond hair is limp, and his face is long and thin, and his smile, although gentle, seems fragile.

"You have a nice place here," Brad says. "Do you find it easier to write in the country?"

"I'm not sure," I say. "I find it easier to live in the country. I guess maybe it's easier to write here, too."

"Just don't try to talk to her while she's writing," Marly teases. "She pretends she's listening, but really, she doesn't hear a thing you say."

"That's not true. I almost always stop and listen to you."

"She can parrot back what you've said," Marly says, "but she's not truly engaged."

"Well, why are you trying to talk to her while she's writing?" Brad asks.

"Hey, you're supposed to be on my side, not my mom's!"

"I'm on the side of the creation of art," Brad says. "You wouldn't want someone bothering you while you're trying to shoot. Besides, Marly, from how you are, it's clear that your mom must not have neglected you too much."

While Atom and Brad browse my CD collection, I sauté the tofu patties until they are browned and crisp and Marly cooks and drains rigatoni and mixes it with butter, basil, and grated cheese. Then we bring the patties, pasta, and salad to the table. There is plenty—Brad, Marly, and I eat small-to-medium portions, and Atom finishes off the rest.

After we clear our plates, we move to the living room. Brad sits on the middle of the couch with Marly and me on either side of him, and Atom stands behind us, looking over our shoulders. As Brad opens his portfolio, I notice the soft spot between the thumb and first finger of his left hand; it is scratched raw, like Marly's was in high school before she started taking medication for anxiety.

The first photo is of a city street at dusk, steam rising from a sewer grate. The streetlights are fogged as if by giant puffs of breath, and the edges of buildings are blurred by the darkening sky. "I'm experimenting with pairing words—just a few words—with each photo," Brad says. He turns the photo over. Handwritten in red ink across its back is:

> Let us go then, you and I
> When the evening is spread out against the sky
> Like a patient etherized upon a table

"Now that seems kind of unoriginal," Brad says. "A too-easy pairing. But I've left it for the time being."

The next photo is of an abandoned kitchen in Pullman. "I took this one about three years ago, with Atom and Marly," Brad says. Shot from above is a porcelain sink, veined with cracks and splashed with dark stains. Below the sink, shattered dishes cover the floorboards, some of which are missing. On the back of the photo is written:

> And I felt
> a strange calmness then
> like my body was already
> falling through the floor.

The third photo is a recent one of Marly wearing a slinky black dress, hands folded on her lap, lips both playful and serious, eyebrows raised. Rather than linger over this photo, Brad quickly flips it over.

> Happiness ... maybe we can learn it, like the rules of any
>   game with balls.
> This is the proper stance. That is where you hold your hands.

I let out a murmuring sound of approval, and Atom says, "That's really cool, Brad."

Brad begins flipping quickly through the rest of the photos, pausing long enough for us to glimpse the images—more city scenes, more wrecked house interiors, and more Marly, wearing the same slinky black dress—but he doesn't linger long enough for us to read the words written on the photos' backs.

"Hey, slow down," Atom says. "I couldn't read that fast even if I weren't dyslexic."

"Yes, we're in no hurry," I say, wondering if Brad feels deflated by our not praising his photos enough. Or perhaps he feels we paid too much attention to the first photo of Marly he showed us.

"This doesn't have to be a one-man show," Brad says, closing his portfolio. "Marly, why don't you get out some of your photos?"

"Because everyone has already seen most of my photos." She stands up and stretches, arching her slender back, closing her hands in delicate fists. "We should get going anyway," she says. "I have to get up early to take care of the shelter kitties." It's Marly's job to feed them and clean their cages, and to hold and pet them so that they grow accustomed to being handled.

MARLY RETURNS the following Sunday alone to have dinner with me and to do her laundry. A lot has happened in the past week, she tells me. Atom has been hired at Menard's, and Brad has been fired from Literary Lights.

"He was fired?" I say. "He seems so capable. What happened?"

"He's only capable some of the time," Marly says, stuffing her jeans and T-shirts and socks into the washer off the kitchen. "He's changed, Mom, from three years ago. Something is really wrong. He got fired from Lit Lite for setting a desk on fire."

"How did that happen?" I ask.

"He did it on purpose," Marly says.

"Why?"

"No one really knows."

She turns on the washer, adds soap, rinses her hands, and then joins me at the kitchen counter. I hand her an eggplant—we are making spaghetti with eggplant-carrot-pine nut sauce—and return to mincing onions.

Marly tells me what happened: Brad spread glue over the desk and then ignited it with a lighter. He had trouble getting the fire going—the wooden desk began to burn, but the glue didn't. The desk, used by Brad and several other employees, was in a closed room. Another employee walked in while Brad was watching the desk burn and called 9-1-1.

"Why would Brad do that?" I ask. With the back of my knife, I push the minced onions from the cutting board into a hot pan coated with olive oil. The onions sizzle like the sound of rushing water. I turn down the flame.

Marly hands the dark, glossy eggplant back to me, as if

we are playing a kitchen form of football. "I'd rather do the carrots," she says. "I hate the way eggplant feels all rubbery and sticks to the knife."

"Okay, here," I say, passing her the half-dozen carrots I've washed. I pull another knife from the butcher block and begin slicing the eggplant.

"He won't give a reason for setting the fire," Marly says, cutting the carrots into long, narrow strips. "Other than he wanted to see how well the glue would burn. And the scary thing is, he was more upset that the glue wasn't flammable, like it said on the bottle, than that he was burning a desk at the place where he'd enjoyed working for five years, or that he could have burned the whole place down, along with everyone in it. He was actually angry, Mom, at the manufacturer for lying about the product's flammability."

"That doesn't sound like him," I say.

"That doesn't sound like the old Brad," Marly says. "But since I've started hanging out with him again, I've started noticing other things. After he burned the desk and got fired, I finally called Natalie, one of his coworkers—well, an ex-coworker, now—to compare notes. And she said the same thing—that Brad has changed."

"How is he different?"

"Well, just before he got fired, he kept going on about a coworker named Jeremy, calling him evil, saying Jeremy was out to get him. And Natalie says Jeremy has never done anything to Brad. Plus, Brad's been saying his parents are evil, too."

"Have you met his parents?" I ask, slicing the rounds of eggplant into blocky fingers, lining up the fingers to slice into cubes.

"Yes. They seem like totally nice, normal people. Kind of conservative, but otherwise fine."

"Sometimes nice, normal-seeming parents are abusive to their children," I point out, alluding to an earlier conversation: given Brad's dread of physical intimacy, Marly and I have wondered whether he was molested as a child.

"I know," Marly says, "but if Brad was abused, I'm almost sure it wasn't by his parents. They seem so concerned about him. And befuddled. Like Grandma Miriam and Grandpa Bob were about Aunt Davida."

Aunt Davida, my ex-husband's youngest sister and Marly's favorite aunt, died of a drug overdose, probably intentional, when Davida was thirty-eight and Marly was sixteen. Davida, who started life as David and underwent a sex change at twenty-one, had become an accomplished artist, but she suffered from anorexia, substance abuse, and depression. She had said she wanted to be buried with her makeup on but otherwise naked, and she was found that way on her couch, the needle she used to inject the fatal dose of heroin beside her on the floor.

"He's not the same person he was," Marly says again. She leans over the cutting board, slicing the slivered carrots crosswise into miniature squares. "I've been talking with his parents, and we've all been talking to Brad, about getting some help. But he insists there is nothing wrong with him, that it's the evil people who are out to get him who need to stop what they are doing."

"He sounds delusional," I say.

Marly looks up from her mound of carefully cut carrots, pressing the knife blade against the board. "Why do creative people always have to be so crazy?"

"Not all are," I say. "I'm not. You're not."

"Yeah, but you're not exactly casebook normal, Mom, and I'm on medication."

⌐

MARLY DOESN'T ARRANGE to have dinner with me on the following Sunday. Besides volunteering at the Humane Society, she is carrying a full load of classes in the vet tech program at Baker College, and depending on how busy she is, sometimes we get together every Sunday, sometimes every other. On the subsequent Sunday, as soon as I set a pan of lasagna on the table, Marly starts telling me what happened with Brad in the previous two weeks.

He continued to criticize his parents and his former coworker but didn't offer any particulars. They were simply "evil" and "out to get him," and Brad was convinced that his former coworker Jeremy was following him. "And get this, Mom," Marly says. "He thinks that Jeremy is very likely an undercover policeman."

"That's really sad," I say. Steadying the pan, I lift a lasagna square onto each of our plates.

Marly picks up her fork and pokes at a noodle's curly edge. "One day before I realized how bad he was," she says, "we were driving around in his car, and I noticed a copy of *The Catcher in the Rye* on the seat, and I started teasing Brad about how only crazy murderers carry that book around."

"Lots of people read that book," I say. "It's a classic."

"I know, but the guy who killed John Lennon carried that book wherever he went, because it has something in it about Holden Caulfield's people-hunting hat."

"I don't remember that part," I say.

"Well, it's in there. At one point Holden says, 'I shoot people in this hat. This is my people-hunting hat.' He doesn't come anywhere near to shooting anybody in the book, but at least a few nutballs took what he said to heart. Besides that Chapman guy, who shot Lennon, there's John Hinckley, who shot Reagan—Hinckley had a copy of the book in his hotel room. Plus, there's a character in a movie, a taxi driver played by Mel Gibson, who thinks everything is a conspiracy, and he buys dozens of copies. So, here Brad is with this beat-up copy sitting beside him on the seat. I was just joking when I teased him about crazy people carrying that book around as if it were their bible, but he got really angry—he was furious. He told me to never joke like that. Later that night, when he was calm, I said again that I thought he should see a psychiatrist, and he admitted to feeling suicidal. He said he thought of shooting himself, and sometimes he imagined shooting other people. I thought, *He couldn't do that, even if he wanted to—who would be stupid enough to give Brad a gun?* So I wasn't really worried about it. But then a couple of nights later we were taking a shower together, and I noticed a bruise on his shoulder. I asked him where it came from, and he said it must have happened during target practice with his grandfather. And I thought, *Oh, shit.* Then he said to me that he had a feeling that he was going to cause my death. That he didn't want to kill me, but that he was going to end up doing it anyway."

"Marly—" I begin. I want to stress the danger of her showering—and letting down her guard in who knows what other ways—with a deranged young man who thinks he might kill her. But before I can formulate a response, Marly cuts in.

"Wait a minute. Let me finish." She tries to tap her fork on her plate for emphasis, but it stutters and clatters to the table.

"Goddamn it," she says, picking it up and placing it back on her plate. She lifts her arms up as if to stretch the kinks from them, then folds them, her bony elbows pointing outward, and presses the backs of her hands to her eyes. "He was starting to remind me of Mitch. I never told you some of the things that Mitch used to say. Like when he was working at this place that melted down metal in these enormous vats, he would look at me really coldly and say, 'I could get rid of you so easily. I could cut you into pieces and slip you into one of those vats, and no one would ever know.'" She looks down, closing her hand into a fist and bouncing it on the table's surface. "Brad never said anything directly about killing me, and, unlike Mitch, he seemed worried and upset about the possibility of my death, but still, I convinced Brad that he had to sign himself into a psych unit. And he agreed. But he wanted one more night free. So I said he could have one more night."

"That's dangerous, Marly. He said he thought he was going to cause your death."

"He can't, now," Marly says. "Don't worry, Mom, I'm safe. Now let me finish." She resettles her restless hands in her lap, one hand holding the other.

"So he spent that night at my apartment," Marly continues. "I couldn't sleep. I lay next to him for a while—he was totally zonked out—and then I got up and cleaned the bathroom. Then I cleaned the kitchen, from the top cupboards all the way down to scrubbing the floor. Finally, it was morning. We made pancakes for breakfast. And then I drove him to the hospital. He didn't want to go; he didn't want me to leave him there, so I said I would stay with him until they made me go away. And I saw him through the signing in and walked him to the door of the ward. He had changed his mind about going in—he was really scared—but once you sign yourself in, you can't change your mind, you have to stay for forty-eight hours. So I told him I'd come back to visit him, and I turned around and walked down the hall and out. I felt bad about leaving him there, but I didn't know what else to do." Marly has begun rubbing and squeezing one hand with the other, as if to work out a cramp. I'm afraid she's about to revert to scratching herself raw.

"When I went back the next day," she continues, "Brad really wanted to get out of there. Atom had come with me, and we sat with Brad for two hours, trying to convince him to stay. He wouldn't listen to us, he was determined to get out. But in the meantime I had called Brad's parents and asked them to help me keep him in, and while Atom and I were talking with Brad, his parents went to a judge and had him committed. So now he has to stay in until the shrinks say he can leave." Marly lifts her hands to her bright hair and pushes it back from her face. I notice that, although her hands are still small, still the size of a child's, they look older—more defined, somehow—and that they move more deliberately, like the hands of a woman.

"Okay, now you can talk," she says. "I'm done." On the plate I set before her, her square of lasagna sits untouched. I glance down at my own empty plate. I don't remember lifting bites of lasagna to my mouth or chewing or swallowing, but without tasting it, I have eaten every scrap.

"Why didn't you tell me any of this while it was happening?" I ask.

"I was handling it."

"What if he had tried to kill you that night in your apartment?"

"A lot of my apartment mates knew what was going on. If they'd heard one sound, they'd have been there in a flash."

"Yeah, like they were there for you when Mitch kicked down your door."

Marly pokes at an edge of her lasagna, normally one of her favorite foods, as if it were a square of rubber or a vegetable from Mars. "They didn't know the whole story with Mitch," she says. "I wasn't talking with them then. Not like I'm talking with them now."

I don't know what to say. I think Marly has taken too much of a risk by taking on Brad by herself. But, as she said, she has handled it.

"So, now you don't have to have a heart attack, Mom," Marly says. "Because Brad's locked up, and I'm safe." She smiles sadly, and her lip twitches as it used to do when she was a child before she began to cry. But the rest of her face stays smooth and still, and her eyes remain dry.

⌒

BRAD IS DIAGNOSED as schizophrenic and made to stay in the hospital for sixty days. Then he comes home to live with his parents. His new medications seem to help, to an extent. He no longer speaks of his parents or anyone else as evil, or of harming himself or Marly or anyone else. Yet he and Marly are no longer close. Marly says the old Brad is gone, and she rarely sees him.

A few more months pass, and Brad starts showing up drunk at Marly's apartment. Marly buzzes him into Madison Manor's once-formal lobby, and Brad makes his way past the grand wooden staircase and the random assortment of shabby couches and chairs, and Marly unlocks the deadbolt of her door and lets him in. She tries to talk him into giving up alcohol—he isn't supposed to ingest any while on his medications—but

Brad persists. He is so drunk at times that he passes out on Marly's couch and spends the night there. Finally, one morning after he wakes up, Marly tells him that he can no longer use her apartment for sleeping off his drunkenness.

One evening I meet Marly in Grand Rapids and we go out to dinner, driving downtown for tapas at San Chez Bistro. It's the first warm day of April, and as we are driving back to Marly's apartment, she invites me to walk with her from there to the library to drop off some books. We park in the lot next door to the manor and walk up the wide, rickety stairs. Marly unlocks the outer door and steps into the lobby. Then she stops abruptly, and I collide into her back. "Mom!" she says, annoyed. But she also sounds alarmed.

Brad is facing us, sitting on a lobby couch—one of the manor's other residents must have let him in. He seems to be in a half stupor, his eyes bleary yet bright. I almost don't recognize him. His thin face has turned puffy, and he has gained fifty pounds.

Brad stands up from the couch. Once nimble, he is now ungainly. He looks at me dully, as if he doesn't know me; then, looking at Marly, he says, "Oh, good, you're here."

"We're not staying," Marly says. "My mom and I just stopped by to pick up my library books."

"Well, I'll just take a nap on your couch then, till you get back, all right?"

"No," Marly says. "I told you I don't want you showing up here drunk and using my apartment to sober up."

"I'm not drunk," Brad says. "I've only had a couple drinks."

"No, Brad," Marly says. She hasn't moved toward her door—the strong door with a deadbolt that the apartment manager put in after Mitch splintered the door made of paneling.

Brad stumbles toward us and stands between Marly and her door. "I'm not sleeping out in the hallway," he says. "What if someone finds me?"

"No one is going to hurt you, Brad," Marly answers, her voice soft.

"If you won't let me in," Brad says, "I'll just leave."

"Did you drive here?" Marly asks.

Brad turns away without answering and starts toward the lobby door, but Marly's little hand reaches out, quick as a bird, and clamps his wrist. She stands holding him tightly in her grip. I adjust my stance, ready to leap between them if he tries to harm her. Brad pulls his arm back, but Marly's fingers and thumb continue to clench his wrist like a manacle. "Give me your keys," she says.

Brad sighs, shakes his straggled hair out of his eyes, and with her other hand Marly dips into his pocket and fishes out a set of keys. She slips the keys into her own pocket and lets Brad go. He is swaying on his feet as if he's forgotten why he's here. Marly turns away from him quickly and opens her door. The two of us slip in, with me walking sideways so I can keep an eye on Brad.

Once inside, Marly lifts a stack of five books and balances them on her hip.

"Are you sure you want to go back out there?" I ask.

"Yes," she says, her voice so crisp it almost cracks. "If he wants to keep messing up his life, that's his option. But I'm not going to let him screw up mine."

We go back out in the hall. I follow Marly across the lobby as if she were the mother and I the child. Brad hasn't moved. Marly does not pause as she passes him. She doesn't pause on the porch, but walks swiftly past the couch where she brought a blanket to the homeless man sleeping there long ago. Years from now, after Marly has married and moved to Florida, she will visit Brad, still living at home with his parents when he is not in the hospital, on her trips back to Michigan. Sometimes Marly will go alone to see Brad; other times she'll bring her husband and their young son. But on this April evening, I follow her down the worn, paint-peeled stairs of Madison Manor and out onto the sidewalk, and she turns toward downtown with her five library books circled in the crook of her left arm. I keep pace with her. We are silent. At the corner, she stops and says, "Can you hold these for a minute?" I take the stack of books, and she zips open her purse and pulls out her phone. "I'm calling his mom," she explains, scrolling down and then tapping a few keys. "Doris?" she says. "This is Marly. Brad's in the manor lobby. Yes. He's drunk or high or both. I took his keys away. I'm not sure if he's going to sleep on the couch in the lobby, or what. Yes. No. That's okay."

Marly claps shut her phone, holds out her hands to me for her books.

"I'll carry them," I say.

Marly shakes her head impatiently. "I can carry them myself."

"Well, why don't I carry half?"

She shrugs and lifts three of the books from the top of the stack of five I am holding, and we resume walking. It's a beautiful spring evening, with daffodils blooming up by the foundations of the elegant, dilapidated old houses, forsythia about to burst into yellow stars, purple crocuses already beginning to fade. Marly's eyes are wet. I want to offer her something: a tissue, a hand on her shoulder, some appropriate words. But I think what she wants most from me is nothing at all, so that's what I give her, looking at the ground as we descend the cracked, crumbling pavement, slanting down and away from the manor toward town.

Love Again

WHEN I FIRST SEE SAM, I'm not looking for a man. It's the first morning of my family's annual reunion, and my two oldest brothers and I have cleared our breakfast plates and sorted our silverware and stepped outside the dining hall. The three of us are sitting along one of the camp's boardwalks, chatting in the sunshine and looking out over Lake Michigan, when a very tall man walks by, wheeling a blue bicycle. The man has dark hair touched with gray at the temples, and he is stooped forward a bit, his long arms reaching down to the bike's black-taped handles. That the man is handsome registers but just barely; my gaze rests more on his blue touring bike. I sold my own red hybrid eight years ago, after injuring my hip while riding. "I wish I could ride a bike again," I say to my brothers as the man wheels the bike past.

"Maybe you should give it another try," Mike suggests.

Arthur folds his arms with a crafty smile. "Maybe you should give *men* another try."

"Oh, *men*," I say. "I don't need another man. Not this week, anyway."

The man with the bike is part of the group with which my family is sharing the camp. When we first arrived, I asked a frizzy-haired, smiling woman wearing a nametag with a little butterfly sticker on it what her group was about. She said they were a splinter of AMUUSE, the Unitarian singles group that has been coming to the camp in Saugatuck for decades, and that this new group was started when some of the AMUUSE singles got married. "The unmarried AMUUSEers didn't want married people in the singles group," she said, "so we started this group for everyone, married people *and* singles. That's why we call ourselves 'Saugatuck for All.'"

For all, I thought as she walked off, *well then maybe there'll be someone here for me.*

But I want to spend this time with my family, not combing through this AMUUSE-ing group that my new boyfriend and I made fun of more than twenty-five years ago, when I first came to this camp to work on the staff. The AMUUSE singles seemed pitiful and desperate to Ray and me then—so old, yet still unattached. It seemed to us that you should have a partner sewed up by the time you started to sag and wrinkle, and that if you didn't, then you should just forget about it. But now the current crop of single men and women, despite their lined brows and baggy throats, no longer look so old, and it is the smooth-skinned staff that gives me pause—they look like teenagers, hardly more than children. Which is, of course, what most of them are, and what I was, when I first came to the camp to work and live.

The next time I see the tall, dark-haired man, he is without his bicycle. I look up from the salad bar, and he looks down at me, and our eyes meet and some kind of current passes between us. This time his handsomeness registers, as well as some sort of deeper appeal. I can tell by that current, and by the glint in his eyes, that he's glimpsed something he likes in me. But I don't want to start anything with a man who lives so far away—all of the people from Saugatuck for All are at least from out of town, and many are even from out of state. Besides, I have only these six days to be with my family, whom I don't get to see very often. I want to spend this week relaxing with my family, not chasing after some stranger.

But I keep looking up and finding him in my line of sight. He is more than a head taller than me, so I see his nametag, **SAM**, with a little flower next to his name, before I see his face. Is the Kalamazoo River safe to swim in? Sam wants to know. Is there a local taxi service? Somehow he's found out that I live in the area. "I don't have a car," he says, "and I'm planning to take the bus back to Ann Arbor. Do you know how to get to the Greyhound station?"

"Well," I say, "it's a little complicated. I can write it down for you, later. Or I can show you on a map."

The following morning at breakfast, when I look up in the foyer of the dining hall, Sam is smiling down at me, map in hand.

I tell him I can't show him right now. "I have to pour milk for my nieces and nephews," I explain. I heft the gallon jug. "But I'll show you sometime."

The light goes out of his eyes and his smile dissolves.

"I'll show you before you leave," I assure him.

Just before lunch, out on the boardwalk, Sam appears again, without the map. He always seems to materialize near me suddenly, as if by magic. "Is it supposed to rain this evening?" he asks.

"I don't know," I say. "I haven't heard any weather news lately."

"What do you do in Saugatuck?"

I tell him that I drive a bus for a local company and that I am also a writer, and he names several writers he likes. We talk some more about books. Then I ask him what he does in Ann Arbor.

"PhD in mechanical engineering, composing and playing music, comedy improv, cartooning," he rattles off. "I do a monthly cartoon for the *Ann Arbor Observer*. I also write short articles for them. Writing articles isn't usually considered creative, but I think it can be, don't you?"

"Oh, definitely, any kind of writing can be creative," I say.

"But humor, whether spoken or written, is my favorite mode of expression." He beams, and I smile back at him. He asks me more questions, and we chat about writing, music, politics, and whatever else comes to mind.

The next morning as I'm waiting in front of the dining hall for the breakfast bell, Sam appears and leans his body against the railing across from me. "What do you think of Jack London?" he asks, folding his long, lean arms across his chest.

"I haven't thought of him in years," I say, "but *Call of the Wild* was one of my favorite books when I was a little kid. Oh, and in high school, we read that depressing little story about building a fire."

Just then, a woman from the Saugatuck for All group stops next to Sam and asks him if he knows where the aromatherapy workshop is meeting this morning. I size her up: she is wearing a long, tie-dyed skirt with a matching top and has an average body and an ordinary face and an overly eager manner. Sam is wearing sandals, baggy shorts, and what appears to be a thrift-shop shirt—it's a bright orange-red and of a cut no longer in fashion, but it flatters his large, lean frame and looks good with his dark hair. Sam tells her that he's not sure where that particular workshop is being held, but a list for all the workshop locations is posted in the dining hall. She thanks him and then asks him what he thought of last night's alternative lifestyles lecture. Sam says he didn't end up going to that. It seems the etiquette here is that of a weeklong party: just walk up and cut in without regard to the previous conversation. But maybe the tie-dyed woman feels it's me who is trespassing, since I'm talking with Sam although I don't belong to their group. She seems more interested in conversing with Sam than he is with her, but he is exceedingly nice about it, and yet he doesn't lead her on. They chat a little more, and the woman walks away, and Sam turns back to me. "I'm not a huge fan of London's writing," he says, "but I thought you might be interested in him from what you said yesterday about your interest in socialism. London was a socialist. And he lived an incredibly intriguing life. Do you know very much about him?"

"No, nothing, really, except that he spent a lot of time in the Yukon."

Another woman passing by stops beside Sam and asks him if he is going to her workshop this morning on hot stone massage. He answers politely that he is not going to make it to that. This woman, dressed in jeans and a plain white blouse, is prettier than the other one, and she seems both more confident and more pleasant. She remains by Sam's side, as if waiting for him to say something further. When he doesn't, she asks him where and when he is holding his workshops, and he says he canceled his creative technology workshop because no one signed up for it, but his comedy workshop will take place in the lodge tomorrow at two. She pauses as if waiting for something more, and Sam waits, too, smiling kindly yet not flirtatiously, making it clear, as gently as he can, that he is not interested in pursuing their conversation. The woman gives up on trying to engage him, at least for now—she says something about maybe seeing Sam at a workshop later today and then walks off, and Sam turns back to me.

That afternoon and evening, Sam walks up to me twice and mentions titles of books that he thinks might be similar to the memoir I am writing, which tells the story of when I quit high school and took off to live in the woods. I've found myself talking more than I usually do about my writing and my personal life to someone who is still pretty much a stranger to me.

⌐

BEFORE BREAKFAST on Friday, I am sitting with my daughter and all four of my brothers on benches near the boardwalk leading into the dining hall, and Sam is sitting on the nature center porch, not too far off. Our gazes meet, and I smile at him and lift my hand in a little wave.

"Call him over here," Zachary says. "We want to interview him."

"Call who?" Mike asks.

"That man who's been stalking our sister all week," Arthur says.

"Are you getting a new boyfriend, Mom?" Marly asks, craning toward the porch.

"Would you guys be quiet?" I say. "It's only someone I've just met."

"Which one is he?" Marly asks.

"I'll point him out later. *Stop staring.*"

"But I'm leaving right after breakfast!" Marly has to get back to her job assisting a vet in Grand Rapids, so she is leaving the reunion a day early.

Dan says, "It's the tall, dark-haired guy who looks like Frank Zappa. I hope he's saner than Zappa. I hope he didn't name his kids Moon Unit and Dweezil."

"He doesn't have kids," I say. "And will you all quit *looking over there?*"

"Invite him over here, then," Zachary says.

"You just leave him alone until I get to know him better."

"We'll be nice to him," Zachary says, using his Italian gangster voice, grinding his big fist into his palm. "We just want to ask him a few questions."

"I'll ask my own questions," I grumble, poking Zachary's broad, muscled chest. "I'll let you know if I need any help."

After breakfast, when Sam approaches me, I ask him if he minds if my brother Dan and his daughter Greta sit in on the comedy workshop that Sam is leading this afternoon. "They're natural comedians," I say. "They're constantly cracking everyone up."

"Everyone's welcome," Sam says. "Whoever wants to can come."

"I won't be able to make it, because I'll be looking at condos with my folks—they're thinking of moving to Saugatuck, and we have an appointment with a realtor at the same time as your workshop. But if I get back in time, maybe I'll stop by for the end of it."

"That would be great," Sam says.

"And if I miss your workshop, if it's over by the time I get back, would you like to go for a walk on the beach?"

Sam looks at me directly, surprised. Maybe he's begun to wonder if I've mainly been putting up with his attention. The truth is, I'm unsure of what to do with his interest in me, yet I want to find out more about him. Unlike the majority of the men I've been drawn to, Sam doesn't appear the least bit ambivalent. And it seems a positive step that he has approached me over and over, rather than me doing all the work of getting things started.

"Sure, a walk sounds wonderful," Sam says. "What time are you thinking of? Where should I meet you?"

I consider this for a few seconds without coming up with anything.

"How about three thirty on the dining hall porch?" Sam offers. "And why don't we wear our swimsuits, in case we want to go swimming after?"

⌣

AT THREE TWENTY, I glance up from my book to find Sam standing under the eaves of the porch, looking expectant, waiting at a distance that is both intimate and polite. I wonder if he is naturally polite or if he has been trained to it by all the feminists in Ann Arbor. It would be nice to have a boyfriend who has already been softened up by feminists. I set down my book and stand up and join him.

Sam is wearing pale blue trunks and a green bowling shirt. I'm surprised again by how tall he is—about a foot taller than me. I'm wearing khaki shorts over my black tank, and both of us are clutching large, worn beach towels. We've taken only about five steps when Sam says, "Well, to start right off with a deep topic, what do you think about death?"

"Death?" My footsteps slow. *What is it with the men I date?* I ask myself. "I don't think about death much," I say, resuming my pace. "I guess you do?"

"Yeah, I've always thought about death, ever since I was a little kid. But even though I contemplate death a lot," Sam adds quickly, "I'm basically a happy person."

By the time we've touched on the topics of death and happiness, we have started down the bluff leading to what was called Staff Beach during all the years I worked at the camp. Now, I've been told by this year's staff, it isn't called anything; its name has disappeared, except in memory.

A slew of dead alewives has washed up along the shoreline. We walk at the water's edge, picking our way among them, and Sam asks if I know what has killed them. "No," I say. "They used to die because they didn't have enough natural predators, but then salmon were introduced and the problem was supposedly solved."

"And what kind of fish is this?" Sam asks, pointing his toes at a huge decaying carcass.

I notice black spots on the fish's tail overlying a shimmer of pink. "A trout, I think. Or maybe a salmon. And I don't know why it died, either."

We pick our way around more dead fish. I have never seen quite so many. It occurs to me that all these dead fish might be a bad omen. Or maybe, rather than the future, they represent all the men in my past.

"How come you don't own a car?" I ask Sam.

"I'm not destitute," Sam says. "I own my own house—I've even paid off the mortgage."

"Oh, I was guessing it's for environmental reasons."

"Environmentalism is part of it," Sam agrees. "I also enjoy the exercise."

We walk for over an hour, talking about our jobs, our families, our various interests. We mention, without going into detail, that we've been married and are divorced. At one point I say to Sam, "So, you've never had any children?"

"Well, I've had *a few*, of course," Sam says.

I look at him, see he is joking, and smile.

"No, none," Sam says, just to make sure.

We had decided to walk first and then swim, but by the time we get back to the camp beach, the wind has picked up. I've gone swimming the past three days—my first three swims of the year—and the water is still frigid. If I swim now, with the air this cold, I explain to Sam, I'll have to shower for a half hour to warm up again. "You go ahead without me," I tell him. "I can swim anytime."

"Yes, I saw you yesterday," Sam says. "How was the weather in Racine?"

I look at him, puzzled.

"Did you enjoy the sunset from Kenosha?"

I still can't figure out what he is talking about.

"Did you make it to Milwaukee?"

"Oh, you mean because I swam so far out. I usually swim twice as far as that—"

"All the way to Iowa?"

I smile and then laugh. "But with the water as cold as it is," I say, "well, I *was* actually afraid of *dying*. So I guess I do think about death sometimes." Death had also crossed my mind then because I was swimming near the stretch of beach where, twenty-four years ago, I scattered the ashes of my first baby. I'd sailed out in a Sunfish with Ray when I was eight months pregnant with our second child, and leaning out over the stern, I'd opened a handkerchief and released what was left of our first. But I don't dwell on this as I stand on the shore with Sam grinning back at me, his blue eyes steady and deep.

⌒

THAT NIGHT after dinner, sitting around a cleared table in the dining hall, my oldest brother tells me that he went to Sam's improv workshop along with our brother Dan and some of their kids. Mike says that he was very impressed with Sam. "He seems like a *really* great guy," Mike says. "Very kind and encouraging and a wonderful teacher. He was so good at getting people to feel comfortable and open up."

"He's very good at getting people to open up," I agree.

Sarah, Mike's wife, looms near us as she sponges off the table. "Why don't we give Sam a ride back to Ann Arbor?" she says to Mike. "Rather than him taking the bus? Isn't Ann Arbor pretty much on the way to Detroit?" Sam is leaving the camp a day earlier than his group, the same day that our family is leaving.

"It's fine with me," Mike says. "We have plenty of room."

That evening, Mike, Zack, and our sister and their spouses go out to a bar in town, leaving their kids back at the camp with the older ones in charge. Dan and Arthur and I decide to go to the Saugatuck for All talent show, to which we've been invited by Sam and others from his group.

Arthur and I enter the dining hall a couple of minutes late, and this time I see Sam before he sees me—he is walking in right ahead of us. I touch his shoulder, and he turns around. "Want to sit with me and my brother?" I ask, and we find three seats together.

We sit facing the fireplace, flanked by windows that look out on the lake, and wait for the talent show to begin. All the tables in the dining hall have been taken down, and the chairs have been arranged in rows facing the fireplace, with an aisle up the middle. I haven't seen the dining hall arranged like this since I was married here—I haven't seen that aisle, created by blank space and the edges of folding chairs, since I walked up it with Ray almost twenty-six years ago. Now, instead of Ray and I offering up our lives to each other at center stage, I am sitting twelve rows back and off to one side, with my brother Arthur on my left and Sam on my right, about to watch others offer up smaller parts of themselves—a song, a dance, a comedy routine. Before the show begins, I turn to Sam and say, "My oldest brother and his wife said that they could give you a ride to Ann Arbor, since it's on the way to Detroit."

"Are you sure?" Sam says. "It's a little out of the way."

"Mike knows where it is—he used to live there. And I didn't ask them—it was their idea."

"Well, that's a very generous offer. Sure. That will be much more pleasant than taking the bus."

Sam seems suddenly perked up, more full of energy than

I've yet seen him. As each act comes on, he leans down to me and tells me something about the performers. During a ballad sung by a woman with long white hair, I ask Sam, "Didn't you say you make music?"

"I sang and played last night," Sam says, leaning down again. "There were so many people wanting to participate that we had to hold it on two nights."

"Oh, too bad I missed it," I say. "What did you play?"

"A song I composed, accompanied by guitar. I also play the piano, but only in my house."

I imagine standing beside Sam at the piano in his house as his fingers move over the keys. I wonder what the inside of his house looks like and if I will ever see it.

Arthur leaves before the third-to-last act, to put his youngest son to bed. Dan, who was sitting behind us, left even earlier, to help his wife with their large family. I stay with Sam until the end: a group of a dozen people singing a song called "When Will Love Rain Down?" All of them are good singers. Three have sung professionally. After the first stanza, the lead singer asks the audience to join in the chorus, and we do, singing with our full voices, not holding back:

> When will love rain down on us?
> When will love pour down on us?
> When will love rain down and surround us?
> When will love rain down?

Sam has a good voice. During one of the choruses, he switches to a lower register, and his voice sounds even better. I want to climb up onto his lap and into his chest, feel his voice from inside him.

At the end of the song, everyone stands up and claps. I turn to Sam and say, "That was really wonderful."

"Yes, it was," he says. Then he looks at me intently and asks, "Are you sure it's okay to ride back to Ann Arbor with your brother and sister-in-law? A friend is taking my bike back for me, but even without it, I have a lot of luggage."

Baggage, I think. *Well, at our age, we all have a lot.* "I don't think it'll be a problem," I say, "but I can go ask. Do you want to come with me and talk to them about it?"

"Sure," Sam says.

We walk out of the dining hall, past the nature center porch, and then over the boardwalk bridge, which spans two high, wooded dunes. From the road below, the bridge looks like an old railroad bridge, with many layered sections of crossed four-by-fours and upright supports, but when you are walking on it, you don't notice that the regular boardwalk has become a bridge unless you look to the side and down—only then do you see that the road below has dropped far away and that you are walking high in the air.

Fifty feet past where the bridge changes back into boardwalk, we stop, and I knock on the door of Mike and Sarah's cabin. Mike assures us that they have plenty of space in their car, and he and Sam talk quietly for a few minutes, Mike's eyes shining in the darkened cabin as he reminisces about Ann Arbor, where he went to college thirty years ago. Then Sam and I walk back down the boardwalk and over the bridge.

I've walked over this bridge thousands of times. I've hauled cleaning supplies over this bridge, to clean the cabins after the campers were gone. I've shoveled snow from this bridge after winter storms. I've walked over this bridge with my dogs, now long dead, with my husband, long divorced, with

Marly when she was a toddler, now grown and living on her own. A week after I first moved to the camp, Ray stood with me on this bridge and pleaded with me to spend the night at his cabin. I'd spent my third, fourth, and fifth nights in his cabin, in his bed, and on my sixth night at the camp, I decided that I wanted to spend a night in my own cabin, sleeping in my own bed, with my assigned, female cabin mate in the next bed over. Ray asked me why; he thought that maybe he had done something wrong.

"I don't know," I said. "I think I just want to be by myself for a night. I'll come back tomorrow night," I offered. But Ray continued to plead, and since it was so important to him and, I thought, not that important to me, I gave in. I slept with him every night after that, except the few times that one of us was out of town, until our marriage ended eleven years later. Occasionally, I've wondered what might have happened if I had followed my inclination to walk away from Ray that day and claim a separate space for myself. Probably I would have returned to him the next night. But I'm not sure.

Now, as Sam walks beside me, I listen to our feet resounding on the wooden boards and realize that it doesn't matter anymore, what I have and haven't done. Despite the deep and lasting sorrow surrounding the death of my baby daughter, the years of my marriage weren't wholly bad—in fact, from this distance, I can see that a lot of my life then was good. And the most important thing about my past is that it must not have led me too far astray, since I mainly like where I seem to be heading now.

After Sam and I cross the bridge, we pause and face each other, expectant yet a little shy. We are standing where the boardwalk splits off in two directions. One branch leads to the cabin in which Sam is staying, and the other leads to the part of the camp where my cabin nestles against a dune. I'm thinking about giving Sam a hug good-night when he says, "Can I walk you to your cabin?"

"Yes," I say, and we continue around the dining hall and to the walkway leading to what had always been the director's house, until this summer. My father-in-law was the camp's director during all the years I lived at the camp, and when I arrived this year and learned that his former house had been turned into a camper cabin and that I and others of my family would be staying in it, I walked through the rooms feeling like one of a race of conquerors. Not that my in-laws had been my enemies—sometimes I even loved them—but there had been plenty of tension between us, especially when my marriage to their son was failing.

We stroll to the end of the walkway and stop, looking out to a line of trees and the lake. Closer in, just beyond the section of walkway where Sam and I are standing, is the location of my ex-mother-in-law's former garden. It's entirely gone now, the irises and lilies taken over by nondescript native plants, mostly dune grass with a smattering of sassafras saplings. The demise of Miriam's garden gives me an odd and slightly evil feeling of pleasure. I can remember the approximate outlines of where the garden once flourished, but someone new to this place wouldn't even guess that it had existed. The past has entirely lost its foothold here, and the present—this very night—is lying on top of it.

I turn to give Sam a good-night hug, and he opens his arms, and we embrace. Rather than pulling away, we linger together. Then Sam leans his back against the boardwalk railing and squats down so that he is closer to my height—it's as if he is sitting on an invisible chair, with his anaconda-long arms wrapped around me. "Are you comfortable like that?" I ask, leaning over to see what his butt is resting on: nothing, apparently.

"Very comfortable," he says.

Although it feels right to be standing near my former mother-in-law's vanquished garden, I feel less sure about standing here with Sam. As we linger with our arms wrapped around each other, him massaging my back and shoulders with his hands and I tentatively doing the same to him, I feel a little uneasy. I hardly know him—what if he turns out to be too touchy-feely? Or too something else I haven't yet imagined? Or not enough in some way? Plus, he is definitely more handsome than necessary—better looking than my second-most-recent boyfriend, and at least as handsome, if not more so, than my last. Too bad Sam's looks aren't more average, so that other women wouldn't find him so appealing. With the exception of his slightly grayish teeth, Sam's face is enticing in every particular, from his huge, inquiring eyes to his strong cheekbones and nose, to his full lips and his kind and generous smile. Add to that his thick, dark hair, his tall, lean body, and his engaging personality, and he is the kind of man whom women flock to.

But just because they flock doesn't mean he will fly off with them—all of my brothers are handsome and engaging and, as far as I know, faithful to their wives. And it would be a shame to reject someone because he is too desirable.

I decide to not kiss Sam in case I change my mind about him later, but after we've hugged and talked for a while and he moves his lips to mine, it seems that it's maybe a good idea after all. Kissing doesn't have to mean that we are committed in any way, and besides, I am liking him more and more. Maybe he can and will become my boyfriend. Ann Arbor isn't that far away, and now that Marly is grown and living on her own, I'm not as tied to Saugatuck as I used to be. I can spend as many nights out of town as my job will allow, and I can eventually even quit my job and move away, if that's what I want to do.

Sam's kiss feels nice. His lips are soft and warm and his mouth is open. I open my mouth and press my lips to his and kiss him back. He is still leaning against the boardwalk fence as if sitting on an invisible chair, which brings him down near my level, just a few inches taller than me.

"How many times have you been in love?" Sam asks, his long arms wrapped loosely around me.

I'm getting used to Sam's big, personal questions—first about death, now about love. "I'm not sure," I say. "I fall in love pretty easily."

Sam draws back and looks at me seriously, his eyebrows raised. "And how does it turn out? Crash and burn? Or do you stay friends?"

"Burn, mostly. Although with my most recent boyfriend, I've stayed friends. We broke up a little over a year ago. Hal makes a better friend than he did a boyfriend. With the one before him, he said he wanted to stay friends, but I was too hurt." My voice, to my surprise, wavers just a bit. "What about you?" I ask. "How many times have you been in love?"

Sam looks thoughtful. "Five," he says. "If you include my first, unrequited love, when I was fifteen."

"And you said you were married once but didn't have any kids."

"Yes."

"How long did your marriage last?" I ask.

"Nine years."

"And how long have you been divorced?"

"About eight."

My counselor would be overjoyed with these numbers. "When was your last relationship?" I ask.

"It ended last fall. We lived together for two years, and we were together for a long time before that."

My counselor would think that Sam needs more time by himself before getting involved with someone new. But I'm not going to pass up Sam based on anyone's statistics—if I wait for the recommended year or two to pass, some other woman will have snatched Sam up and latched onto him for good.

"What are you looking for in a relationship?" Sam asks. "What kind of relationship do you want?"

"One that lasts," I say. "One that will last the rest of my life."

"Wouldn't you get bored? Wouldn't you miss the rush of a new relationship, all the excitement?"

I feel the muscles in my shoulders tighten. "No," I say. "I like routine. I mean, I don't want things to be exactly the same all the time, but I'm basically a creature of habit. I don't get bored easily. And I'm sick of saying good-bye to people. To men."

Sam clears his throat. "Well, I'm a party guy," he says, "a pure playboy, out to get whatever I can." He waggles his head in an imitation of coolness. I look at him swiftly, a little startled, pulling back, partly involuntarily and partly so I can see him more clearly. He has already resumed a serious expression. "I want a relationship that lasts, too," he says, gazing at me directly. "It's not all black and white, I know. You give up, but you gain. Someone said that marriage is like a golden cage: those who are out of it, want to get in, and those who are in

214 · Lisa Lenzo

it, want to get out. But I think the deeper treasure lies inside." He continues to gaze directly into my eyes, and I feel that same current, only stronger, as when our glances first met. "I want to go deep," Sam says. "I want the depth that you get from being with the same person for a long time."

We kiss some more. Sam has risen from his sitting-crouch, and now that he is standing again, he looms high above me. I had meant to find a shorter man this time, for my hopefully last relationship, so that we could kiss standing up without my neck getting sore, so that all of our body parts would match up when we lay down together; instead I've gone in the opposite direction. But other than that, kissing Sam has begun to seem like a very good idea.

⌒

SAM'S BREAKUP SPEECH is delivered to me ten minutes after he walks in my door one Friday evening, as I stand on my couch with my arms around him; because Sam is so tall, I've acquired the habit of hopping up onto couches and chairs to make our heights more even.

"I have something serious to say," he says.

"Uh-oh," I respond, seeing it coming.

He looks sad. Then he tells me that he's decided to end our relationship because I'm not funny enough. "I love you more than I've ever loved any woman, and you're the best match I've ever found, but humor is very important to me."

I shake my head, disbelieving, even though Sam brought up his problem with my sense of humor nine months into our relationship, and then three more times in the nine months since.

"You're serious," I say.

He nods. "I can go home now, if you want," he says. "Or I can stay for as long as you like—whichever you prefer."

"I prefer you not break up with me," I say.

Sam shakes his head.

Another woman might have kicked him out right then, but I think over what I should do, still standing on my couch, still with my arms around Sam, although more loosely. I don't want him to leave without talking it over. But I also don't feel up to mooning around the house, uttering painful sentences with long pauses between them, so I say, "Why don't we go skiing"—this is what I had planned for us to do, when I thought we were going to have a regular weekend together—"and we can decide what to do after."

⌒

Two hours after Sam has broken up with me, we are sitting in The Everyday People Café, formerly known as The Douglas Dinette. It's my favorite restaurant in Saugatuck and Douglas, my adopted pair of hometowns, where I've lived for so long— almost thirty years—that rather than six degrees of separation between everyone else and me, there is often not even one. At the table to our left is Steven, one of my former bus passengers who many years ago did me the favor, when Marly brought home a young Siamese that didn't get along with the other cats, of adopting the outsider kitten. Across the room from me is Len, a local librarian who knows my taste in books. And to our right is Vic, the realtor who showed condos to my folks a year and a half ago, when they were considering moving to Saugatuck. Someone who isn't too observant might look around this restaurant and exclaim, "Annie, look at all these men! Forget about that long-distance thing with Sam!" But

Saugatuck is known as the Provincetown of the Midwest, and almost all of the male diners here who are single, including Steven, Len, and Vic, are also gay.

Vic and I wave at each other, and then Sam and I return to trying to decipher the menus without our reading glasses. I call across to Vic, "I keep forgetting I need glasses, now that I'm getting older."

"Try mine," Vic says, and he leaps up and hands them over, and I slip them onto my face.

Sam and I have stopped at the café for dinner because skiing made us hungry and I didn't feel like preparing dinner for a man who is leaving me, but I also didn't want to send Sam on a three-hour drive on dark, snowy roads back to his house in Ann Arbor without his having had something to eat. I suppose I could have fixed him a baggie of crackers and cheese and kicked him out, but I couldn't bring myself to be that harsh to the man who, for the past year and a half, I've been considering the love of my life. And besides, I'm not convinced that Sam will follow through with his intent. I haven't decided whether I want him to spend the night, and, if he does, whether I want him to sleep in my bed. But whatever we end up doing, we need to eat at some point.

Vic's glasses only make the print blurrier, so I hand them back. Sam's eyes are bad enough that reading glasses are a necessity, but mine are more borderline, so I remove the blue glass shade from the candle lantern and read the menu aloud to him by the flickering flame. The waiter stops by our table and tells us the about the specials—plank-roasted salmon and duck with ginger *gastrique*.

"Why don't you go ahead and get the duck?" Sam says after the waiter leaves, even though, at twenty-four dollars, the duck is one of the priciest items on the menu. Encouraging me to choose an expensive entree is out of character for Sam—back when we first met, when he was still in that stage of trying to impress a new lover, he nevertheless turned us away from an Ann Arbor restaurant after reading the window menu on which prices averaged fifteen dollars. "We can eat well for cheaper than that," he said. This from a man with his mortgage paid off and over a hundred thousand of his engineer's salary and consulting fees in the bank. But I was pleased I'd found someone who was frugal with his finances rather than drowning in his debt.

I go ahead and order the duck—why not have a duck fling on what might be our last night together? And considering the guilt Sam must be feeling and that he's urged me to get it, he'll probably offer to pay for it. After the waiter leaves, I reach across the table and take Sam's hand. I don't yet really believe that he wants to give up my touch. I'm feeling more confident than is warranted, I guess—I still think I can coax him back. And we sit like that, holding hands with me wondering if he wants such contact or is just putting up with it.

From two tables over, Vic spots our hands and catches my eye, and, repressing his more usual raunchiness, he calls across to me: "It looks like love!"

I grin back at Vic sourly and say, "It *looks* like it," unable to refrain from blurting the truth, even though I don't want to admit it to myself. Vic and the male friend he is sitting with look slightly shocked.

"Appearances can be deceiving," I say, and despite this hard fact, my face is composed and my voice is even and strong. I still feel I can turn Sam around into staying with me. My counselor would call this denial, and say that by literally hanging on to Sam, I'm attempting to avoid the inevitable break, but people can and do change their minds in the middle of things, or even at the end of them. Meanwhile Sam is shrinking in his seat, a difficult and uncomfortable feat for a man of his height. I'm sort of glad that he is suffering a little, but I don't want to prolong his awkwardness or mine, so I withdraw my hand from his.

Before an uneasy silence can set in, Sam asks me if I know the theory of relativity. It's a strange question to be asking on a last date, and I wonder if Sam is bringing it up now because I've recently confessed to him that, due to major gaps in my education, I am scientifically and mathematically illiterate.

"No, I don't know the relativity theory," I admit, as the water boy, who went to school with Marly, fills our glasses. "Hey," I say to Jordan, who nods and smiles back. If only breaking up, if that's what we are doing, could be this simple: topping off glasses, exchanging smiles, moving on to the next table. I'm afraid of how I think this breakup will really play out: an overarching, painful sadness lasting for weeks or even months.

"Do you want me to explain relativity to you?" Sam asks, looking at me across the flickering blue candle lantern and the white butcher paper.

I hesitate, wondering if he is trying to be helpful, to teach me something I'd like to know, or if he just wants to create a safe distance between us so as to prevent awkward silences, doleful looks, and recriminations. It's hard to lash out or look doleful when you are frowning in concentration. "Sure, go ahead," I say. I might as well get something out of what might be one of our last conversations.

So, slowly and carefully, Sam launches into the theory

of relativity. "The first thing you need to do is put aside your assumptions about time," he says. "And keep in mind that everything about relativity is strange but real." Fitting the tips of all eight of his long fingers together, he leans in closer, although he still seems distant, sitting across from me on the far side of the table. "Imagine you're on a spaceship," he says, "traveling at the speed of light. The speed of light is constant—it never varies. But time changes—it's relative—depending on the speed you are traveling."

Sam continues to explain the theory, and I'm pretty sure I am grasping his meaning, but then at one point I realize that I am just looking at him, watching his lips and hands move, without hearing what he is saying. "Wait a minute, back up a couple of sentences," I say. "I zoned out for a minute."

Sam patiently backs up and starts in again, politely making sure that I am following. "The faster you travel, the slower time is. For instance, if you were traveling at the speed of light, time would stand still." He pauses, lifting his eyebrows a little.

"That doesn't make sense. It sounds like the opposite would be true."

"It is counterintuitive," Sam says, "but that's how it works." Then he tells me that no one has actually proven that time would stand still, because no one has yet traveled at the speed of light.

"So, if it hasn't been proven, how do they know it's true?"

"Because they've figured it out mathematically. They know enough to know that if we could travel that fast, it would be proven."

"So, they're just *assuming* it's true. I always assumed relativity was a certified fact. Well, damn! Now I feel cheated."

Sam looks uncomfortable. Perhaps he fears my feeling

cheated by the unproved theory of relativity will segue into feeling cheated by his shaky theory regarding his decision to leave me. He starts defending his mini-lecture, saying "that's just one aspect," and "research gives clear support," and something about how scientific theory is far weightier than vague, laymen suppositions that are also called theories, but I guess he finally sees by my sour face that he's lost his audience. "Excuse me, I need to use the men's room," he says, rising up from his chair, looking as tall and gawky as Abraham Lincoln, but far more handsome.

Well, *what if Einstein was wrong?* I want to call to Sam's receding back. But Einstein was Einstein, after all. I figure this is not a case of the emperor having no clothes and no one wanting to admit they can't see his invisible finery, but something more like the time when Marly was thirteen and we were driving home at night on two-lane country roads, and I kept dimming my headlights at each oncoming car, then switching them back to the high beams after the car had passed by. I'd clicked the dimmer switch a dozen times—click, click, click, click, click, click, click, click, click, click, click, click—when Marly, in the passenger seat, as ignorant about the mechanics and relevance of dimmer switches as I was about Einstein's most famous theory, turned to me and snarled, "Will you pick one setting *and just stick with it?*" I tried to hold back my laughter, but it bubbled up out of me.

Remembering this incident, I think of something I once said to Sam, in defense of my sense of humor. The world is funny enough, without its even trying. Besides the abundance of unintentional humor that leaps out at me from my daughter, from strangers, from billboards and TV ads, there is the fact that, while I was growing up, two of my brothers were comedians and the other two were also fairly funny, and someone needed to be their straight man, or rather, their straight girl. All my life I've been surrounded by humor and absurdity, and it has seemed silly to try to add very much to what is already a surplus.

Sam doesn't want just an audience, however; he wants someone who will meet his humor with more humor. What doesn't make sense is that if having a jokester for a partner is that important to him, then why didn't he break up with me a few weeks after we met? I've asked him this, and he has enumerated the many other things he likes about me. "And I fell in love with you," he says. "But when it comes to spending the rest of my life with someone, I know I need someone who will joke with me a lot."

The waiter sets down our plates, and as I wait for Sam to return from the men's room, I cut into my duck and consider, as I have before, whether I could be funnier if I tried. But not having made humor a major component of my life, I don't know if I could pick it up now, plus I don't want to feel as if I'm auditioning for a part. And I remember what my counselor has said, that I should hold out for a man who will love me as I am. Anyway, I think what is really bothering Sam is my reaction to his women friends, in particular our last disagreement regarding Suzanne, who is lively and pretty—none of Sam's women friends are ugly or even plain—and who has lamented to Sam at least a few times in the six months she has known him that her boyfriend will only have sex with her once a week. I've asked Sam to meet Suzanne only in public, for lunch, and Sam has agreed to this. But then three weeks ago he told me that he had accepted an invitation for Sunday brunch, just the two of them, at Suzanne's house. "But she wants to show me her indoor garden!" Sam protested when I reminded him of his promise.

"Yeah, I'll bet she does," I answered.

As the blue candle lantern continues to flicker, I poke my rice with my fork. When Sam said to me, five months after we met, "Someday I'm going to be extremely attracted to another woman—I'll refrain from becoming physically involved with her, but I want to be able to pursue her as a friend," I considered calling off our relationship. But I reasoned that, as Sam fell more deeply in love with me, he would set aside this errant notion and commit to me in full. And a song Sam started writing soon after we met helped quiet my fears. He kept adding more verses and playing and singing it for me at the piano in his living room; then he started recording it in his basement studio. The song was about how we met and the early days of our courtship, and it contained a couple of lines that made me smile: "It is I who pursued her, she reminds me all the time," and "She claimed she could swim all the way to Iowa." But the line that stilled my fears was the refrain, repeated over and over: "Got to find a way to have her near me all the time / Got to find a way to have her near me all the time."

At first Sam and I talked about either one of us moving—Sam to Saugatuck, or me to Ann Arbor—but we came to agree that I would likely be the one to move, since I could more easily find another job. I'd miss Lake Michigan and my friends, but I'd be closer to my family who live in Detroit, and I could come back to Saugatuck to visit. Rather than drive a bus in Ann Arbor, I thought I'd work at a daycare or a bakery. And maybe I'd occasionally teach a writing class at U of M. But now, according to Sam, those plans are no longer on the table, those dreams are up in smoke.

Sam returns from the men's room with a composed face. After he resumes his seat, I ask, "Are you canceling our relationship because I insisted you cancel that brunch date with Suzanne? I'm wondering if that's really the reason."

Sam's face sinks. But his voice purrs out smoothly. "Annie, this has nothing to do with anyone else."

"Not necessarily so you can have sex with Suzanne, but in order to replace me with a girlfriend who won't try to limit your flirtations with other women?"

"Why won't you believe that this is about my need for humor?"

"Because every time you've complained about your need for humor, it's right after I've complained about your need for other women. Like when that woman you met in that resale shop offered to show you how to do yoga with ropes."

Sam waves his fork through the air in front of his face as if to distract me, or maybe it's to deflect the questions and accusations I am flinging.

I stab into the side of my duck. "You shouldn't have waited five months to tell me that you were going to be extremely attracted to other women. You should have let me know that *before* we had sex."

Sam looks around us to signal that others might be listening. I look around us, too, at the faces of Len the librarian and Steven the saver of kittens. Len is involved in his own conversation, which seems to be progressing more smoothly than mine, but Steven glances back at me in commiseration. Vic the realtor, who had said, "It looks like love!" is now frowning at me in dismay.

"Next time a man calls himself a playboy, even if he's supposedly joking, I'm going to throw him off the bridge—or at least run the other way! And with your next girlfriend," I say, pointing my knife at Sam, "don't include any of that stuff about marriage being a golden cage and the deeper treasure lying inside it. Just tell her, right from the beginning, that you intend to pay a lot of attention to other women. Tell her you're not necessarily going to have sex with other women, but you might want to try yoga with ropes!"

Sam stares back at me with his mouth hanging slightly open. I turn my knife to my plate and sink it into my duck, slice off a piece of juicy, dark meat, and shove it into my mouth. Sam bends to his roasted salmon, his eyelids hiding his eyes.

Sam finally finished his song about us more than a year after we met, and he made a final recording last month and gave me a copy for Christmas. It turned out differently than I thought. I was disheartened and a little frightened to hear his laughter right after each chorus, as if his loving words were just a joke: "Got to find a way to have her near me all the time" was followed by his hollow, zany laughter. Perhaps he was just exhibiting his wacky humor, I told myself, listening to his wild, unfeeling voice. Or maybe he was distorting our experience to make the song come off as hip. But in my heart I knew there was more to it than that. And it didn't matter that he'd decided, after a drink or two with the yoga-with-ropes woman, to not take her up on her offer. Whatever he felt for that woman, and whatever he feels for any other, the strength of what he once felt for me has faded.

⌒

WHEN THE BILL arrives for my duck and Sam's fish, Sam picks up the folder. I offer to split it with him.

"No, I'll pay," Sam says.

"I'll get the tip, then." Usually we either split the bill or take turns, and Sam has never turned down my offer to pay the tip.

"That's okay, I'll just put it all on my card," Sam says, guilt getting the best of him, I'm sure—first the duck, and now the entire bill.

"You should break up with me more often," I say.

"That's funny," Sam says, smiling sadly.

⌇

WE DRIVE BACK to my house, and I tell Sam that yes, I still want him to spend the night. I'm still not ready to believe that he will leave me for good. What about the greatest sex he's ever had—or so he's claimed—and what he calls my great, rich brain? He once hinted that he is at least a low-level genius. So, if he's so smart, I think as we let ourselves into my house, why has he made such a stupid decision?

We get ready for bed, brushing our teeth in separate bathrooms, and I remember a snatch of interview I once heard on NPR that has stuck in my mind: A biographer of Einstein was asked, "Don't you think you were a little rough when, in describing Einstein's personal life, you called him an emotional imbecile?" "No," the author said simply. "Those are strong words," the interviewer persisted. "I know," the author said. "I chose them carefully."

After I've finished brushing my teeth, I change into a T-shirt and underpants and meet up with Sam, who is already in bed. I lie down beside him with my back to him and pull his arm around me, and as he silently strokes my shoulder, I say to myself what he has told me on other nights when I was fretting about one thing or another: *Put all your worries outside the bed. No worrying allowed in the bed. Make this bed a worry-free zone.* Then, trying to think of something pleasant that isn't connected to Sam, I imagine sandhill cranes flying over my house; I see their wide wings and stretched necks and wait in the silence for their creaky cries. They are gone for the winter, but they'll be back in early March, just over a month from now.

I wake at three in the morning and get up to pee. When I return to my bedroom and see Sam sleeping there, my first inclination is to slip back in beside him and cozy up to his warm body. Instead, I carefully lift my two pillows and walk to my writing room. On the floor, folded in half and pushed to one side, is the covered piece of foam I slept on in my little apartment right after my marriage ended. Then the foam mattress served as my bed; now I use it for company and naps. It still has the same green fabric cover I sewed for it decades ago. I unfold the foam mattress, pull a sleeping bag from the closet, arrange it on the mattress, and climb into the bag. Lying awake with my eyes closed, I try to feel strong. But I can't help dreading the vast expanse of space and time—seemingly wider than Lake Michigan, longer and deeper than I can fathom—which I will have to get through before I'll feel all right again.

I resettle my head on my pillows. I wait for sleep. I don't know yet that this is the last night Sam will spend at my house, or what I'll find tomorrow, when I ski down to the lake by myself. I don't know yet that tomorrow I'll discover something unexpected.

I'll start out on the main trail that leads to the beach. The trees on either side of me will be pillowed with white. I'll ski through the woods on deep snow.

I'll ski hoping that Sam has not left me for good, yet I'll tell myself that if he doesn't come back, then I won't have to move to the other side of the state; I won't have to leave the lake and the woods, my friends and my house, this place where I've made my life. Still, my chest will hurt and at the same time feel hollow.

Where the tunnel of woods opens out, I'll pause above the beach and look out at the lake's ridges—three sets of them formed by ice hills strung together. Beyond the farthest ridge, I'll see hundreds of small icebergs, bobbing and floating all the way to the horizon.

I'll sail down the high dune to the snow-covered beach, then take off my skis and wander out onto the frozen lake, swept clean by the wind, and gaze at the formations spreading and rising all around me: high hills covered with a shiny glaze, crusty balls scattered at my feet, glittering icicles hanging like rows of fangs from the edges of frozen cliffs. Suspended in the ice I'll notice separate grains of sand, specks of brown and black and gray, and I'll wonder, as I have before, if some of the specks might be ashes, strewn by me and by others, before me and since.

I'll have climbed down inside a cone of ice shaped like a volcanic crater, and, kneeling at the center of this rounded hollow, I'll be looking down through a further opening, a narrow crack in the ice, when this thought will come to me: *I have my life, and I'll have love again. Not with Sam, but with someone else.* And I'll kneel there on the ice, feeling the cool burn of the winter air on my cheeks, gazing down through the crack and wordlessly breathing my thanks: for the world all around me; for the life I am living; for the love that is coming.

ACKNOWLEDGMENTS

Without my writing pals, these stories might still be searching for their final forms: thank you Andy Mozina, Bonnie Jo Campbell, Joan Donaldson, Glenn Deutsch, and Jane Ruiter.

Thanks to Jim Daniels, for permission to use lines from his poem "Hold Up," and to John Rybicki, and in memoriam, to his beloved wife, Julie Moulds, for the use of part of Julie's poem "Playing Catch."

I've shared much pie, cake, tea, and laughter with my circle of women friends, who listened to many of these stories before I transformed them into fiction.

I still remember my early teachers, Richard Deemer and Sandra Simon, and I continue to refer to and rely on my later teachers, Stuart Dybek and Jaimy Gordon.

I couldn't have hoped for a better or kinder crew than

everyone at Wayne State University Press, and I'm grateful to the Saugatuck-Douglas Interurban Transit Authority for providing me with a steady job that allows me time to write.

Thanks to my big, wide family, especially to my mother and father, for their steadfast love and support, to my daughter Cloey, without whom these pages and my life would be lacking in a thousand different ways, and most of all to my husband, Charlie, who enriches all my days, and without whom this book and my personal life would still be a work in progress instead of satisfying and complete.

"Still Life" was published in the Spring 2007 Prize Issue of *Mississippi Review* as "The Yellow Linoleum."

"Aliens" was awarded an honorable mention in *Glimmer Train*'s Fall 2009 Family Matters Contest and was a finalist in the 2013 contest at *The Bellevue Review*. It appeared in *Brain, Child*'s special issue on teenagers in spring of 2013.

"Strays" won first place in *The Georgetown Review* contest for 2013 and was featured in their 2013 spring issue.